Oper

Brimstone Press

My thanks to June Clifton for her help,
to Mike Richardson of New Zealand for the
front cover, and to those countless people,
strangers & acquaintances, whose ears
I've bent over the years.

Opening Gambit

Journal One of Brother Spikus U.M.

A Story of Hystærical Significance

Narrated by **Clive Russell** with the help of
his friends and other odd people!

First published in 2008 by Brimstone Press
PO Box 114, Shaftesbury SP7 8XN

www.brimstonepress.co.uk

Author contact: spikesdad44@hotmail.com

Designed by Linda Reed and Associates,
Shaftesbury, SP7 8NE
Email: lindareedassoc@btconnect.com

Printed and bound by CPI Antony Rowe,
Eastbourne

ISBN 978-1-906385-11-8

Preface to 'Opening Gambit'

It's the 1950s and the location's a small shop in a run down complex at Preston Park beside the Brighton Viaduct. The barber has just brushed off, and seen out, the last customer of the day who was an elderly gentleman with a very unusual breed of dog.

The door sign is turned around, the chair covered with an old sheet and then, when reaching to switch off the mains, the barber notices a paper carrier bag nestling down beside the steps. It contains a small package securely covered with a canvas wrapping. He naturally assumes that it belongs to the old chap, as it wasn't there at the mid afternoon sweep-up, so he hangs it on the hat-stand fully expecting the pair to call in the next day.

But it was never reclaimed and ended up in a cabinet drawer that inexplicably locked itself from that day on.

Fast-forward 40 plus years. The barber has long retired to Hastings and his shop, together with the surrounding area, is earmarked for re-development. A demolition firm from Andover strips and guts the buildings and anything saleable ends up at the Friday Night Auctions in Salisbury.

My particular interest started when I found the package whilst rummaging through the boxes beneath the bookseller's stall at the Sunday Market at Harnham. The journals sewn into the canvas cover intrigued me and I subsequently traced the path of the contents from Brighton to the Salisbury Auctions. The bookseller, who had bought the cabinet together with a boxlot of books, eventually broke open the drawer and sold the package on to me completely unaware of the contents.

I deem myself most fortunate to have been the chosen one.

The journals related to events at Salisbury Cathedral during the 16th century and were translated, from the original Latin, by a convalescing Royal Marine Officer. He was wounded leading a skirmish at the port in Canton during the 2nd China Wars and it was in a bombed-out dock building, whilst waiting for help to arrive, that he discovered the original journals.

I have narrated the first part of the story beginning with the auction as related to me by the Market Trader, then the results of my own enquiries around the Preston Park area, and finally to a somewhat wasted journey to the Royal Marine Museum at Portsmouth.

With the help of my friends and other odd people I have then used the information from the journals, plus researched material from the Cathedral and other sources, to construct the story, within a story, into a more readable book form.

The Acquisition

Salisbury, October 1997

The usual early morning booties with their charity shop ensembles, and firmly shut handbags, crowded around the latest arrival at the Harnham Car Boot Sale. I quickly set up the tabletop and, even before the first box was laid out, most of the noses had drifted away leaving only those with an interest in the written word.

Items in good condition were authorbetically arranged in old plastic trays while the rest, mainly old and broken print books, despondently awaited a rummaging through by the dealers in this field. These were randomly scattered so, if one fell and broke a bit more, then it really didn't matter!

Trade was quite brisk until a couple of Canadians, talking loudly and standing central, were rooting through the books and thereby stopping others from looking. I told them to either buy something or move on so they chose the latter which enabled the regulars to resume their orderly browsing.

An elderly gentleman, on his knees under one of the trestles, then discovered a package squirreled away at the bottom of a box. An old book maybe was sewn into an oilskin cover and he held it aloft to ask the price.

He caught me unawares and I tried to think where it had come from.

Then I remembered and my mind zoomed back to that Friday Evening when, in the auction hall across the way, I very nearly lost out in the battle of Boxlot 91.

'Lot 90. This small kitchen cabinet with drawer. 1930's in solid oak. Somewhat battered which, may I say, adds to the charm and this piece is most suitable for restoration.'

The carrier wrestled to open the drawer but without success.

'A touch of soap on the sliders will soon fix that. Now what am I bid?'

'Only fit for firewood,' commented some wag.

'Do I hear ten?'

'Somebody give me five. Come on, first hand.'

There was no response so the auctioneer consulted his sheet as the carrier made a quick decision.

'Two for one. Same vendor so we'll put it with Lot 91.'

'Good idea George,' said the auctioneer and continued.

'Lot 91. We have a box lot of assorted books, some good, some not so good and in need of a little tender loving, but all very readable so what am I offered?'

The auctioneer's eyes scanned the crowd searching for a nod, a wink, a twitch, a hand or any indication of interest but he was disappointed.

'There's some nice old books, money-spinners, start your own bookshop! A do-it-yourself bookbinding project for the wife in the winter. What about ten?'

'Pence,' suggested the same wag.

'Come on, cabinet and books. Five measly pound for the bargain of the evening'

'Five? I'm not going any lower.'

His theatrical gesture of incredulity brought uncomfortable shuffles from a few of the closest regulars who bought almost anything but there wasn't a murmur.

He looked down at George. 'What do you think, pass it in?'

'Two!'

My bid was loud and clear before the carrier had time to answer, as my mind rejoined its body after a flight of fantasy into Mrs Bickerstaff's boudoir. I'd somehow wandered off, mentally, at the crucial moment just before Lot 91 had arrived on the podium as it contained one particular book that had taken my fancy.

'Please be patient Sir, I haven't even stated the lot number yet.'

His voice boomed out, loud and clear, from the high position and he evidently enjoyed its ring of authority.

'For the boxlot,' I replied rather sheepishly, 'Lot 91.'

'I'm sorry Sir; we are on to Lot 92 so you must have lost count.'

A few sniggers followed his comment but I'd suddenly become the focus of attention from the rest and I was buggered if I'd back down.

'You were still on Lot 91 when I bid!'

'I beg to differ Sir but I had announced the next Lot.'

'No you hadn't!'

Everybody and his dog now had me in their sights. The auctioneer looked at his watch, whispered something to the carrier, and then announced. 'Come and see me after the auction Sir.'

'I put in a bid before the Lot was closed so have I got it or not?'

'The Lots were combined and it's not high enough.'

'Mine was the only bid for whatever and you're compelled by law to accept.'

'Not if there's a reserve on it.'

'Well is there one?' I asked.

A few of the old auction hands were muttering and one regular, a chair restorer called Harold, voiced his support. 'For Christ's sake Dennis, sell him the bloody lot so we can get down the White Hart for last orders.'

'Well is there one?' I repeated and waited for his reply.

'Lot 91 sold to the terrier in the army jacket. Your number Sir?'

It was bucketing down outside and, while waiting in the loading bay, a voice asked if I wanted a hand. The boxlot with the kitchen cabinet, an unexpected bonus for which I had already planned to convert into a bookcase, sat loaded on a trolley.

'That's very kind of you,' I replied to the stranger standing at my side, so we waited until the rain stopped before wheeling my purchases into the car park.

'It won't fit in there,' he observed sizing up the cabinet and then the Beetle.

'Look,' he continued as the heavens opened again. 'Let's put the lot in my van and I'll drop it off tomorrow. You live at Stapleford don't you? It'll cost you a tenner.'

That's how these Good Samaritans turned predators make their money. Looking out for punters like me with big ideas and small cars.

'Could you pay me now? Just in case you decide not to be in!'

I thought, momentarily, to ditch the cabinet but decided against it and gave him a note of the address together with the rest of my weekend's beer money.

'See you tomorrow then.'

'About what time?'

'Early morning.'

I waited, somewhat anxiously, all that fabulous English Autumn Saturday for my delivery to arrive while cursing myself for being so stupid as to think he meant today. And I should have taken the Mrs Beeton book out of the box while I had the chance.

He finally arrived though, together with a drunken mate, late in the evening after the pubs shut. For openers they backed into the fence, setting off Horace the Hound and waking the neighbours, then carefully unloaded the cabinet that had somehow sustained a broken leg since the previous night.

The drunken one expected a tip, it was obvious from his hints, but I moved the cabinet against the shed, covered it with a waterproof sheet, then carried the boxlot inside the house and made myself a cup of tea. A few moments later I heard the engine start and peace descended once again around and about.

That night the heavens opened and when the alarm clock went off I'd already decided to give the market a miss. A few minutes later I got up and went to the window to find the sheet had blown off in the night and that wag's remark at the auction came to mind.

'Only fit for' was the phrase he used about firewood and it fitted as my eyes alighted on the twisted heap of timber. After breakfast I went outside to inspect the sodden remains and found the top piece had split with the structure obviously beyond repair so I commenced demolition there and then with a crowbar.

The jammed drawer eventually gave way and a paper bag burst forth revealing something book shaped, wrapped in an oilskin, and tied with oakum twine. As my plans for the bookcase had been carelessly terminated I stuck the lot number ticket onto the package and laid it to one side before carting the old wood to the local dump for someone else to use or burn.

In the lounge I set up the folding table and inspected the books. The dampness intensified the musty smell so I lit the gas fire and laid the books along the hearth.

'Puddings and Pies. Mrs Beeton's Handy Reference Book Number Seven.'

This was the one I was after and still in good condition for its age.

I had examined it before the sale as some prospective purchasers, those without my deft touch and roughly rummaging through the book boxlots, sometimes tear the dust covers and thereby diminish the value. The bookshop's ink stamp, from Shropshire, was inside the front cover together with a Daily Mail bookmark. I was pleased with my purchase and laid it to one side for further perusal.

The rest of the consignment was comprised of an incomplete set of 1950's encyclopaedias, the 'Story of the Desert Air-Force Volume 1', a few Newnes Engineering, a parcel of 1940's 'Aero Model Maker' magazines, and some paper backs on rose growing.

I turned the oilskin wrapper over and a loose corner revealed two or three leather bound journals that looked water damaged.

Then the phone rang.

It was my son asking if I could help him with some plumbing in return for which he would treat me to a Sunday pint and lunch. A good idea so I piled the books, and the package, back into the box and carried it through to the garage to join the other boxes of books destined for sale, on my stall, at the next Sunday Morning Boot Fair.

'Well. How much is it and this airforce book as well?'

His question brought me back to the present and one of the Canadians was asking something from the other end of the stall.

'A pound each will do,' I answered and soon the purchases, nestling within a Tesco's bag, were handed over and the old boy went on his way whistling the aria from *Mozart's 41st*.

The Perusal

The contents of the bag were dusted off in the garden before being allowed into the house where a space had been cleared on the desk and clean newspapers laid out.

When I tried to slide the journals out of the cover however they started to tear so I turned them over and found a seam of twine sewn along one edge. It was only when I cut the stitches and pulled out each individual thread that the oilskin loosened its grip on the contents.

They were notebooks, smaller than an A5 and covered in ancient leathercloth, to form a roughly matched set. The fourth one was bulkier with a dust cover of chart paper. Very old chart paper and I read, written on the cover;

Stickman of the South Pacific.
My sketchbook; 1859-65.

I flicked through it. Lots of pencil and pen drawings of churches, crosses and bells with numerous notes. On the frontispiece was written;

William Stickman—Soldier of Fortune and
Layman of the Clothe.

An analysis of this particular book would take time so I placed it to one side and opened the first of the smaller books to read the old script title before continuing;

Das buchs ab der Brooter Spikus und Otters.

'The original journals were discovered in a bomb-damaged building that sheltered me until help arrived. Memories of that dreadful day filled every subsequent waking moment with the nights passing in drug induced euphoric visions. *The Admiralty Manual of Therapeutic Suggestions for Damaged Marines* was unearthed from the archives and dusted off.

Navy Surgeons had suggested some simple therapy to help clear a troubled mind so various projects and tasks were selected, placed in front of me, but my enthusiasm soon waned. Just how many phallic shaped bed warmers for lonely sailors' wives was I expected to knit?

Having always enjoyed languages and the classics, I commenced translating the journals and this kept me occupied until my return to England. Some of the leaves of the original journals were torn or water stained with the writing faded in parts. However it was generally in a readable condition so I took it upon myself to sympathetically add when the storyflow was interrupted by the aforementioned damage.'

It was signed with an address; *'Lt William Stickman. R.M.L.I., 10th RM O/A Raiding Party. HMS Acorn. Canton. China Station—1857–8.'*

I paused here to make myself a cup of tea and a sandwich, cheese and tomato with a sprinkling of sea salt. Some pepper, no butter. I checked in my *'Timetables of History'* and found that in 1856 the British fleet bombarded Canton and then, in 1857, a combined British and French force captured Canton. So if a Naval Hospital had been established ashore it must have been in 1857 but a Prize of War or a Hulk could have been used for this purpose.

What I'd read so far had the makings of a good story and an interesting winter project in the offing. My humour is offbeat and people need to take time to get to know me but few bother. The unusual appeals so, with my stronger glasses, I scrutinised the first few pages and found another scribbled footnote;

'At this point notes seemed to be in various scripts by various beings and their inclusion is essential for the storyflow so the future chapters will cover these idio-syncrasies.'

Then the phone rang. It was Muni asking if I wanted to join her for *'Pensioner's chicken with stir fry'* as she had shopped at the PSS (Pensioner's Special Stall) at the market where there are some good buys, all very cheap, but one has to eat them on the same day as the produce always seems on the verge of going off.

I declined and made do with a Cup of Soup and a hot cross-less bun from the market. The baker on the stall had told me that the crosses had somehow ended up on the doughnuts in the next tray and would I like some hot cross jam doughnuts?

'No thank you,' I said, 'it just doesn't sound the same.'

After reading for an hour or so all I've got written down is the preface.

The Journal of Brother Spikus and Others.
Rome – September 1528.

'This journal begins in 1528 when the Holy Roman Emperor, Charles V, using German Lutheran, French Bourbon, and Spanish Protestant troops, had the Pope, Clement Vll, under siege in St Angelo's Castle in Rome.

Charles was displeased with the authority Clement had given to Cardinals Campeggio and Wolsey as Legates at the divorce hearing of Henry Vlll. The Queen, Katherine of Aragon, was an aunt of Charles and as he already cared for his mother, Joanna the Mad, he did not want to be saddled with her distraught sister as he'd enough problems as it was.

Existing in St Angelo's at this time was a mouse. Not an ordinary mouse but one destined for great things. His name was Giovanni and he was a Vatican ChurchMouse.'

The story opens with his decision to emigrate by hiding away in the Cardinal's portmanteau, then the coach trip across France and the boat trip to England. On arriving at Salisbury Cathedral he has an unexpected encounter that leads on to an appointment as a casual cleaner with the *Exouris* which is the A.B.C. (Ancient Brotherhood of Churchmice.)

This was just the start of his adventures so could it be true or could the originals be a figment of someone's overactive imagination? Maybe an allegory as a huge number of hidden meaning treatises, texts, messages and scripts were circulating around that era particularly amongst the oppressed intellectuals.

England's religious thinking had started to swing when Henry bent the rules and pubic opinion carried it further. Martin Luther rebelled against the *Indulgence Tax*, as it funded a lifestyle of decadence for the hierarchy within the Vatican, and then in 1517 he posted his 95 theses on the Church Door at Wittenberg Castle.

In 1520 Leo X excommunicated the heretic with his bull named *Essurge* which Luther publicly burned. It seemed a cruel thing to do!

For this theory to be credible one would then have to link account happenings in the journal to important dates in the religious calendar with humans substituted for the mice. One name does spring to mind, that of 'Erasmus'

Dear old Desiderius Erasmus. Erasmus. Erasmouse! Surely not.

Could slipping an 'o' between the 'm' and the 'u' then adding an 'e' be the key?

And then Erasmouse could be substituted for Anonymouse?

There was even a mention of letters that Brother Spikus, using his later title, had written to the Corinthians on a variety of subjects but I couldn't find any further details. It was after two a.m. when I reluctantly laid down the journal, closed the cover, and went to bed.

Since then I've found deciphering the strange writing quite difficult but from this, and research at the local library, I've narrated the story of a little known and largely forgotten band of brothers whose heroic deeds were woven into the rich fabric tapestry of life during the turbulent times of Henry VIII and his good Queen Katherine.

These were *The Exouris,* an abbreviation for – *The Ecclesiastical Others.*

Histœrical Note

'Last I do vow that mine eyes do desire you above all things.'

Katherine penned these words in a letter to Henry, shortly before her death.

She was originally his sister in law and the Vatican had granted a dispensation allowing them to marry but Henry, now suing for divorce, wanted this ruling reversed. The reigning Pope ordered a Vatican Cardinal, one already holding the absentee bishopric of an English diocese, to attend the London proceedings in an effort to put the Ecclesiastical Spanner into our Judicial Works.

Cardinal Campeggio excelled in the area of appearing to do everything, while achieving nothing, and this inaction followed the Pope's orders to the letter.

'Summum et maximum mandatum,' which means what it says.

It took a year to get the proceedings under way and a further six months before Henry took the law into his own hands. He set about loosening the Papal yoke that held England in check and added the title, *Defender of the Faith*, to his screen credits and then, on November 14th 1529, his Excommunication arrived in the morning post together with a clerical warning for the lovely Anne B.

Our story starts a bit before the above date so find a quiet corner and read on.

The Search

The following weeks, after reading and digesting the first journal several times, I became curious regarding its origin.

Beach's, the old and well-established bookshop located in Salisbury's High Street, had finally closed its doors and the treasures within were sold off. The building waited, shuttered up and shut down, until a new owner arrived on the scene and the shop finally gutted of any unwanted remains. This act of vandalism had occurred a few weeks before I bought the books and I initially thought that the journals may have come from there but I was mistaken.

The oilskin wrapper had a Lot Number and the airforce book an ID Ticket used where a numbered auction lot has several items. By cross matching the ID Ticket's date and the Lot Number, together with a certain amount of phone subterfuge, I obtained the name of the Vender who had entered certain articles for sale on that particular day.

This turned out to be a large demolition firm from Andover so I took advantage of a free morning and arrived at the firm's gates well before lunch where the foreman, a nice chap named Sid, took pity on me. I was the first struggling old writer who had ever wandered into his yard and he even went down into the archives to emerge with the 'Where things come from and go to' book.

The firm had stripped and gutted some buildings close by the Viaduct along the Preston Road in Brighton. The cabinet had definitely come from a barber's shop and he was sure that the books came from the same place because a bundle of R.A.F. Association posters were stuffed down the side of the box which he later gave to the Air Cadet Unit at the local school.

This last statement, possibly linking the parcel with the R.A.F.A. posters and the boxlot, sent a slight shiver down my spine. Unfortunately he couldn't help me further, having only done the one trip down to bring back a lorry load of material, so I thanked him for his time and arrived home in the afternoon to search through the other book I had bought at the Boot Sale.

Nothing was written in the front pages of 'The Story of the Desert Air-Force Volume 1' but inside I found a newspaper clipping of the Brighton and Hove R.A.F Association contingent in the 1953 Remembrance Day parade. There was a group photo underneath, and a caption, but I had no idea who I was looking for so I gave up and made myself a cup of tea.

Another week passed before my curiosity was aroused again so I took advantage of a cheap day return to Brighton travelling via London where I had a document to sign. With that business quickly concluded I continued on to Brighton and was soon standing by the Viaduct awaiting that intuitive gut feeling which indicated the direction of the buildings or the barber's shop.

A small newsagent and a transport yard came into view as I approached from the out of town side so, walking under the bridge whilst looking to the left, an empty lock-up shop with the transport yard's name over the door came into view. I carried on down into the yard and spoke to a desk clerk who told me that the shop had been a barber's but it was empty when they had leased it a few years back.

He didn't know the barber so I thanked him for his help and returned to the shop. I peered through the window, imagining the posters on the wall, but it was all such a mess that I gave up and wandered further up the road.

Hunger dictated that it was well past lunchtime and then a thought struck me. If the barber was in the wartime forces then he could well have enjoyed a pint so I scouted around, in a circular fashion, for the nearest pub and a little way up Argyle Road I found 'The Engineer'.

I walked into the lounge bar, ordered a pint and a steak pie, then asked the barman if he lived locally and whether he remembered the barber's shop under the bridge.

He did and he didn't but an old boy, earwigging in the corner, did.

'I knew him ever so well.'

I walked over and asked the barber's name.

A few shakes of the head later and the name was still on the tip of his tongue.

'Roy, or Reg and he used to come in Friday lunchtimes.'

He quickly finished his pint so I bought him another and sat down at his table. This turned out to be a good investment as I learnt that Roy, or Reg, had served in the Desert Air Force during the war and he even pointed him out in the newspaper cutting. However a few years ago, so the old boy said, he retired from barbering and moved to Hastings near his daughters.

He went on to recall many anecdotes of the Friday lunch-time crowd, which he related as they came to mind, before starting on one about a peculiar dog named Ecclestone, his elderly owner, the barber's cat named Harry, and a parcel.

The last item, the parcel, obviously sent a stronger shiver down my spine.

Evidently one of the barber's customers had left a parcel and never returned to collect it. The barber, after a few days, put it into a cabinet drawer that inexplicably jammed itself and it would have meant breaking through the underside to free it.

'Had the barber ever mentioned what the parcel contained?' I asked.

The old boy thought it was some old books but the drawer stayed jammed from that day forward. This was one of the barber's favourite stories that always ended with;

'I really must get that drawer opened!'

This time the spinal shiver increased in its intensity, maybe it was the way I was sitting or the effects of the pie, as this revelation most probably linked the journals with the barber's story. However he could add nothing regarding the identity of the owner of the parcel but he did remember that Ecclestone belonged to an unusual breed.

I was most grateful and bought him another pint before leaving to head towards Brighton Pier where, in a sunny corner sitting on a deckchair, I wrote down the bones of the old boy's recollections of the barber's reminiscences'.

And here they are;

The Prologue

'Are you cutting pensioners' hair today?'

Roy, or Reg, switched his attention from the captive head to new blood.

'Come in, come in, does your dog need a trim too?'

The captive head sniggered as the barber, on reflection, watched the old chap plus an even older dog, settle into the shop corner.

'That's a weird looking creature,' he further reflected as the canine eyes seemed to bore straight through the mirror and into his own.

'Straight neck or taper?'

Translating biag, [British industrial answering grunts], was an essential skill the barber had picked up over many years and it enabled him, on this occasion, to concentrate on the job in hand. A shift to the left side of the chair, in order to comply with the reply, moved him out of the dog's sight-path.

'Leave the sides long?'

Yet another grunt so, lifting the neck hairs, on the slant, the shears soon scissored the desired effect and the closeness between artist and subject came to its inevitable conclusion.

'How's that then, sir?'

The affirmative nod was rewarded by a quick neck wipe, the matadorial removal of the protective sheet, and culminated in one shilling and two pence of the customer's money ending up the shop till.

'And now you, sir?'

The old chap placed his shopping bags carefully in the corner, removed his coat and hung it up on the hook provided, then walked over to the chair.

'Just a trim sir?'

'Not too much off, thank you.'

The barber could sense the dog's inquisitive stare as he assessed the head shape and snipped a few hairs then, moving around to the left side, he finally found a position where he could safely observe without being observed.

Having looked at hundreds of headshapes and faces in his time, he had reached the conclusion that there were only a dozen or so different types of each.

Similar headshapes might have different faces and vice-versa but everybody would fit into one of the twelve squared type frames. Animals fell into the same pattern, but he had never, ever, seen a face such as the one that graced the head of this dog.

It was the teeth on to which the barber's eyes were transfixed.

The bicuspids grew forward from the gums, running parallel with the ground and were not dissimilar to a pair of horns sprouting from the mouth.

'Ouch!'

The lack of barberial concentration had lead to a customerial cry of pain which resulted in a dogerial jump up; it also knocked over the corner chair.

'So sorry sir,' he said and moved across to pick up the chair.

A couple of the shopping bags had tumbled down into the kitchen area so he descended the steps and gathered the parcels back into the bags.

The dog growled as the barber returned.

'Looking at Ecclestone were you?'

'Sorry about that sir, as a matter of fact I was. A most unusual breed of dog if I may say so.'

Another growl but this time at the cat who eye-balled the dog whilst walking slowly from the kitchen. This *'cool'* approach was intended to put the frighteners on the creature that had dared to disturb the Shopcat's late afternoon nap.

Harry was the antithesis of your normal barber's cat who was deemed, by tradition, to be fat, and lazy, and to fart a lot. Nothing fazed this feline equivalent of a Tiger Tank who had limped away the victor after a stand up fight with the Milkman's horse!

'Leave him Harry.'

The barber's request was somewhat unnecessary as the distance to go had been reduced enough for the cat to catch a glimpse of fangsville.

Respect became the key word for the cat to get through this day unscathed.

Ecclestone's tail started to wag as he liked cats; they didn't stand and stare at him for hours as human beings and fellow canines were prone to do. The tail-wagging mode encouraged continuation of the approach, albeit in a gingerly fashion, with the cat rubbing up against the dog's ear on arrival.

'Well,' exclaimed the barber, 'I've never seen him do that before.'

Harry could never see himself doing that sort of thing either but it just seemed the right thing to do at the time.

And it felt good too so he snuggled up to the dog's port quarter.

'What sort of dog did you say it was?' asked the barber.

'I didn't.'

'Well what sort is it?'

'You wouldn't know if I told you.'

'Try me.'

'The initials are E and T.'

'English Terrier.'

'A sort of a terrier.'

'What do you mean 'sort of'?'

'Well it goes down holes but not to hunt animals.'

'Ethiopian Tracker.'

'Don't talk nonsense.'

From that point on the haircut progressed in silence and culminated with the customer being helped on with his coat prior to settling the account. No tip was offered but the business of the day was over and the barber looked forward to his tea.

'I do apologise for my rudeness, but Ecclestone does attract a lot of attention.'

'No harm done sir but I would like to know.'

'He is an English Truffling Hound.'

'I have never heard of that one sir.'

'Questionable practices involving quite intensive interbreeding with the French Truffler have brought this particular breed almost to the point of extinction. Such a shame as they have a lovely nature.'

'Thank you for sharing that sir, I try to learn something new each day and today I have.'

'Come on Ecclestone, time to go home.'

The dog accepted a farewell nuzzle from Harry as they walked towards the door.

'Don't forget your bags sir.'

'Thank you. One of the failings of old age I suppose.'

'Good Evening Sir and thank you.'

'A pleasure,' replied the old chap clipping the lead to Ecclestone's collar who then gave the cat a friendly nod before leading his master out of the shop and under the Viaduct.

'I'm certainly going to break my neck,' remarked the barber to the cat, 'unless I fix this kitchen light.'

The reason for this outburst was a near fall over the step as the barber reached over to switch off the main power at closing time.

'Hello, what's this?'

He leaned over to retrieve a small parcel which had fallen down behind the steps. It felt like a few books and it had evidently been with the shopping bags he had knocked over earlier. No doubt it would be picked up tomorrow so the barber hung the parcel on the hat stand, locked up the shop, and walked home for his tea followed by the cat who was looking forward to his.

A note was pinned up in the window after a week advertising the fact that a parcel had been left and awaited collection but the old chap and, in the cat's view anyway, his delightful dog never, ever, visited the shop again.

Sitting first on the shelf, then on the kitchen cabinet, and finally put into the drawer, the package remained unopened for a number of years.

The barber retired, and then faded away as barbers tend to do.

The cat, under the misguided impression that all Milkmen's horses were pushovers, came off a poor second best with the latest addition to the Milkfloat brigade and the effort popped his clogs.

Then, as we already know, the shop and the surrounding buildings were earmarked for development and the interior stripped of anything worthwhile. The recycling firm carried out the gutting and the kitchen cabinet, together with a box of books, ended up in the Friday General Auction at Salisbury Market Buildings.

Any traceable leads via the barber now seemed exhausted but I knew as much about the parcel as he did. I inquired at the dog club about an *English Truffling Hound* but no one had ever heard of the breed so it was a bit pointless asking if they knew of anyone who owned one.

I did read however that Trudy, a 7 y/o bitch, was entered at Crufts in the *'Over the Sticks'* event but she carried on running through the Main Entrance and disappeared down the tube station escalator never to be seen again.

After the Brighton trip I felt my next, or possibly only other, option was to check out *Lt William Stickman* with the Naval Service Records at Kew but, as Portsmouth was closer, the Royal Marine Museum might well be worth a visit.

The first half of cheap day return whisked me to a city paralysed by a bus-strike so I walked towards the Hard. The 'Overlord Tapestry', depicting the lead-up to the D-Day landings, was on the way so I wandered in and thoroughly enjoyed it.

Further along the path was a sign, 'Royal Marine Museum – 3 Kms'. It was more like 5 miles after which I fully expected to be signed up for a 3-year stint as a sort of *'Thank you for persevering'* award.

On arrival I found the historical information section was shut and anyone who knew anything about anything was off for an early lunch followed by an absentee afternoon. Two young girls, obviously employed to hold the fort, seemed the sum staff total and they were lost in their own world.

I wandered around the exhibitions, finding nothing on the China Wars, until I reached the Medal Section where displays in glass top cases with more below in sliding glass top drawers were on show. Someone had left a unit open and a clipboard, with names and awards written up in columns, sat on the cabinet top.

Crimea War medals, won in the same decade 1854–56, were on display so I slid open the next drawer down to reveal a half dozen or so *'2nd China War Campaign Medals'*. Young Victoria's Head, in silver, on its pink-red yellow edged ribbon lay there together with the dates, all around 1857–8, and the names of recipients.

Pte Booker & Pte I Berry.—Royal Marine Light Infantry.
Cpl J Prettyjohn V.C. & Sgt/Major V Brown. —R.M.L.I.
Gnr J Chamberlain & Sgt R Danke.—Royal Marine Artillery.

The 1st China War lasted from 1854–56 and the 2nd one from 1857–60 and it would have been too much of a coincidence to find Lt Stickman's medals here – but an interesting fact emerged from subsequent research. The crews of HMS Diamond and Albion, forming part of the Naval Brigade, broke through the Walls of Sebastopol on Oct 16th 1854 with the situation dragging on until 1856.

Cpl Prettyjohn won his V.C. in the Crimea serving with this Brigade and, as he had the *'Canton'* clasp to the 2nd China Medal dated 1857, this confirms that the Royal Marines were in Canton and the entries into the journals might just be legitimate. Lt Stickman must have then recovered from his wounds, both mental and physical, either before or during 1859 after which he was well enough to start his sketchbook and sail around the South Pacific.

I wonder if he knew Lt Edward St John Daniels RN. (Stripped of his VC won in the Crimea) and buried in an unmarked grave at Hokitika in New Zealand – There-by hangs a Tale!

A non-striking station bound bus came along at the Museum Gate. I pondered during the journey to the station whether he could have been a career Marine or transferred from the Army or Navy which seemed to be a more popular method around that era. I should try the Kew Archives and find what actual ships, or R.M. units, fought in the Crimea and at Canton. Maybe his Service Records are available, although I haven't his service number, but I'll search online and see what turns up. Anyway, on with the main story ....

Epistle One

Giovanni was born in the Castle St Angelo, a fortified sanctuary used by the Holy See, and was the youngest male in a family of churchmice on the staff of his Eminence Pope Clement VII. The bones of the mouse's illustrious ancestors, found on the banks of the River Tevere, had been carbon dated to indicate roots stretching back to the Emperor Hadrian.

The arrival of the plague drained the last vestige of hope from many of the siege weary inhabitants as conditions like these were all too common in conflicts of the times when, in the glorious name of Christianity, church fought church. This was an internal struggle between factions who should have been collectively kicking with the left foot towards the same goal.

Exouris counselling groups helped with the daily problems but any glimmer of hope was quickly replaced by the horrors of the plague with food shortages adding to the traumas. The rat and cat population of the castle seemed to be thinning down by the day and the mice felt that their turn was not far off.

In this environment of abject misery the mouse became restless, a condition that his Mother identified and then tried to allay with tales of happier days. Of picnics by the river, then dozing in the afternoon sun with Grandma even swimming. Of walks along the underground passages into the Vatican's basement market where the bustle of life, the colours, smells, and dialects, all added up to an experience not to be missed.

The assurances that these times would soon return seemed to help her but it did nothing to change Giovanni's mind. Peace and tranquillity hadn't a chance to develop in the soul of this sensitive mouse who was of the opinion that an ambitious chap-mouse, one who could turn his hand to anything, would have no problems earning a crust elsewhere.

He made the decision to emigrate and, from that day on, kept a sharp eye out for any opportunity to fulfil this quest and get away.

While awaiting his chance he carried a rucsac, containing essential supplies, with him in readiness for the journey. Packed within, amongst various odds and ends, was a small army knife that had fallen from the pocket of a very small Swiss Papal Guard. This essential piece of equipment lay snuggled amongst a change of nether garments, a hair shirt, spare socks, towel, a comb, his toothbrush, and a cheese and pickle sandwich in the event of an emergency.

Every morning he bade farewell to his Mother not expecting to return in the evening although he usually did and she had the tea ready on the table. However on the day in question an opportunity arose and later that day his chair sat empty in the parlour.

'Good Old Charley' was the call from the Emperor's troops whilst a few stalwart souls inside the walls replied with 'Clement for ever'. For the moment diplomacy had taken the place of fighting and various agents were moving freely throughout the grounds.

Giovanni's knowledge of the castle layout, together with a face disguised using black stuff his Mother smeared on her eyelids to attract Father's attention, enabled him to gain access to the Pope's chamber where a conference was in progress. His Holiness sat considering the Cardinal's request that someone else should carry the bulls to England as he had arranged a much-needed holiday by the sea.

'I am aware of all that,' interrupted the Pope, 'but the divorce situation between Henry and his good Queen is deteriorating rapidly. Your particular skills of appearing to do everything, whilst actually achieving nothing, are in great demand.'

Patiently listening nearby to the conversation, and thinking how a visit to England would be just the ticket, the Cardinal's hat portmanteau came to Giovanni's attention. It had an unusual lid, slightly ajar, and this was his chance so he stepped inside and secreted himself under the bottom shelf. The timing was good because the conference soon came to an end with his Holiness blessing and farewelling the Cardinal.

The journey to England began at the Staging Inn outside the Main Gate and this particular Cardinal, Campeggio, suffered acutely from gout. He walked in a dot and carry one fashion so the portmanteau, carried by the valet and his boy, moved at a leisurely pace and seemed to have gained weight but they weren't paid to complain.

With the coach and horses prepared and the ornately sealed Papal Dispatches, plus the personal luggage and the odd case of wine already loaded, the Cardinal climbed aboard and his portmanteau set up in one corner.

The foodsacs were then examined, as he always insisted on the finest of tables and expected the same standard in his travelling hamper, and he was so engrossed in checking the contents that he failed to notice the mouse climbing gingerly from under the lid to a place of sanctuary behind the cushion. A safe and warm place to sleep had to be found so Giovanni, putting his distaste for vandalism to one side, used *the hole-poking in backs of seats* gadget from his army knife and carved out a space in the insulation.

It turned out to be a long and tedious trip and also, with a real risk of Thieves or Customs ransacking the coach at any time, the mouse constantly prayed to his St Christopher's medal. The Cardinal nodded off regularly so when he did, or when the coach was empty, the mouse took sustenance from the sandwiches and quenched his thirst from the rather drinkable supply of Chablis 98 on board. Eventually they reached the coast of France and it was at the port of Calais, whilst unloading the coach, that the valet dropped the portmanteau. The mouse, in his exhausted and fragile state, very nearly cried out but the old leather and silk padding saved him from any serious harm.

They joined the other passengers being embarked on to the ship direct from the smaller boats, together with their luggage, and although the wind had dropped the rough sea left the mouse feeling definitely queasy. He dare not be sick so he lay on his back with feet vertically up against the sides, wrapped the towel around his head, and bit hard on his toothbrush until they were all safely on board.

The Cardinal, in full regalia and attended by the valet, soon departed from the cabin to socialise amongst the other passengers and the mouse waited for a while before he popped his head up to look around. A bowl of water sat within reach and a cotton bud lay nearby so he climbed out and up onto the washstand. The water was still warm and the cotton bud had one clean end so what more could a travelling mouse want?

He stripped down to his nether garments and gave himself a good wash, together with a whisker brush before changing into clean underpants and socks. His trousers and mousecloak benefited from a good shakeout after which he cleaned his teeth, combed his hair and rolled all his toiletries into the towel before returning them to the portmanteau.

The weather had moderated by this time and mouse needed some fresh air so he decided to take a turn round the deck. A large brass hook held the cabin door ajar and he was halfway through the gap when the most awful cat suddenly appeared and took a swipe at him. Striking with the left paw, curved in a standard hooked pattern, the shot missed by a slimwhisker and the mouse backed into the cabin at a great rate of knots.

Ship's cats have retained an extraordinary sense of smell from early gainful sea-going employment on

Viking Ships seeking out the best fishing grounds but unfortunately their former Masters' cruelty has rubbed off on them and they have no respect for mice, church or otherwise. Even clean and friendly churchmice, following their calling in the seaport areas, have to be vigilant at all times.

The cat, looking like one of the Vatican's Mafiamoggies, glared through the gap in the nastiest way but Giovanni's strict ecclesiastical upbringing, together with the fact that he had known some very nice church cats at St Angelo's, enabled him to smile in a benign sort of way that seemed to enrage the cat even more!

At that moment the valet returned with a large brush to sweep out the cabin and, noticing a rather portly feline rump poking out from the door gap, took to it with the brush. He was so violent that it was as if he had harboured a hatred of cats over many years and this time the mouse had great difficulty in keeping the benign smile off his face.

The call for passengers to be ready to disembark sounded after the anchors dropped and the portmanteau, together with the rest of the baggage, was carried up on deck for Customs inspection. This was just a formality and the Cardinal's official party, together with one unofficial mouse, was soon bound for London with an armed escort of soldiers in attendance to ensure a troublefree journey.

There were regular overnight stops at various monasteries where the Cardinal rested and attended meetings. The valet went off to do whatever off-duty valets did, usually with kitchen maids no doubt, and this gave Giovanni the opportunity to explore.

A chance encounter, in the downstairs pantry of one of the Cistercian establishments, led to an invitation for afternoon tea. It was very enjoyable with jolly nice buns and the Monkmouse, together with his family, were most interested in his adventures and made him promise to keep in touch.

Among the Cardinal's Bishoprics was Salisbury where he planned to pick up some legal papers from the Vicar General before moving on to a secure location, somewhere on the Thames, where he would prepare his brief for the divorce hearing. Back on the coach, listening to the Cardinal conversing with clerical advisers, it became obvious that the Royal Divorce, and someone named *Nan Bullen,* were causing serious problems. Giovanni also felt alarmed at the tales of plague and pestilence around London so Salisbury, although he had no idea what it was like or whether the Cathedral needed additional staff, seemed a safer place. He therefore decided to give it a whirl as the name tended to roll smoothly around the roof of the mouth like a jam. Salisbury Jam!

They arrived late at the Bishop's Palace where the luggage was carried up to the Master Bedroom after which everyone seemed to disappear leaving the mouse incarcerated in his firmly shut prison and dying to go to the loo. The oxygen levels were starting to drop and he could feel a migraine coming on so desperate measures were called for.

Eventually the valet arrived to unpack the Cardinal's clothes and lifted the lid of the portmanteau before turning away. Giovanni had just found the *getting out of a leather hatbox* gadget on his army knife but grabbed his pack and took off like the clappers down the main staircase. A polished floor bounced him off a chair leg but he carried on through the kitchens and into the gardens where he gratefully relieved himself against the nearest handy bush.

The Cathedral emerged as he walked, bathed in the ethereal light of the moon, and Giovanni rejoiced in the truly awesome sight that had a simplicity contrasting strongly with the ornateness of St Peter's. But the majesty of the edifice made his whiskers tingle and this encouraged him to stride out the boundaries with a spring in his step.

It was cold though and when he stopped to tighten his belt, put up his hood, and thank the Lord for his thick socks and boots, his enthusiasm seemed to falter and he became increasingly aware of the reality of his situation.

He hadn't a skirrical microgroat of English currency in any of his pockets so when the inns and alehouses of the area closed their doors, followed by shouts, screams, and the extinguishing of candles and lamps, all this added to the descending gloom.

He felt very down in the whisker.

'What am I doing here?'

Repeating the question several times, he then repeated it again to accentuate the syllables.

'What-on earth-am-I-doing-here?'

The need to marshal his thoughts along more practical lines, like finding somewhere safe to sleep, came to the fore and when the inevitable wet-eye started he felt even lonelier and missed his Mum.

A movement from a shadowy doorway caught his attention and, as he turned, the fast evaporating tears made him lose the train of thought. A soft voice locked his kneecaps as the words reverberated through his Y-fronts to dry out in his throat.

'Hello sailor, looking for a bed then?'

The voice continued. 'Lordy, Lordy me, I thought it was one of the lads from the wool barge, I am so sorry your Eminence.'

And the sound materialised into an amply proportioned ladymouse who stepped from the shadows and walked slowly towards him.

Epistle Two

Angelica

S he was freezing her butt off and just about to pack it in when that dishy mouse wandered into view wearing a scarlet cloak. The locals here usually wore grey so she didn't recognise him as a churchy but introduced herself anyway before asking why he was lurking abroad at that time of night. Churchies were always pleading poverty so, when he replied that he wasn't lurking abroad but seeking a bed, she called him a silver-tongued smoothie and added that she would be pleased to help!

There was no reply so the offer was repeated. Still no reply and when a distant church clock chimed the hour of midnight she tried one last time to break the impasse;

'Look love these heels are killing me so could you please take me home!'

It was obvious he needed a little help in the decision-making department so she gave an irresistibly delicious throaty chuckle, then grabbed his arm, and propelled him and his rucsac through the cloisters and on to her pad.

Their dreamless slumber came to an abrupt end when the sound of willow hitting bone, followed by a mournful *Ahhh*, rent the nocturnal stillness of the Close and he leapt smartly out of bed. Just as quick he leapt back in, it was really cold standing on the stone floor in his underpants, and she assured him that the commotion was the Canons Choral settling scores after their drinking sessions and not to get his vicars in a twist.

She struck the flint to the candle and a flame soon glowed as she proceeded to brush her hair and curl the ends of her whiskers. Her smile was most seductive and, when she asked his name, the reply was acknowledged with a loud snort.

'What sort of poofey name is Giovanni? I shall call you Spike as it matches your magnificent mousehood!'

This outburst made him slump back onto the pillow exhausted and he thought how horrified his dear mother would have been at the name Spike.

'Food's on the table and Mass begins in an hour's time.'

He awoke with a start, having dropped off again, but a spiritual black cloud formed from his misery followed Angelica to the kitchen and she returned to ask the reason. Spike then admitted to being an alien, sort of arriving by chance, and she snorted again in reply;

'What do you mean, sort of arriving by chance?'

Spike sniffed, started his tale, and was thankful to see her calming down as the story progressed but this started a wet-eye as he wondered how his mother was managing.

She reached out for him. 'I thought you were one of the French exchange mice. Gerard Du is from Chartres and we have had several others.'

Despite his misery she sensed his whiskers bristling.

'I'm an Italian mouse from the Vatican and travelled over with the Cardinal.'

Faltering he added; 'but he didn't know it at the time.'

She wondered if he had a work visa then assumed the negative and decided on the oblique approach.

'Last week they took a Chinese mouse away who had been working in one of the cafes in town without a visa. You will have to be careful and keep close to the Cathedral ready to leg it inside to claim sanctuary if any of the Immicegration Police come snooping.'

It was obvious that Spike was getting quite agitated whilst dressing as he couldn't find his other sock so Angelica fetched a pair of hers, pink with a knitted Danish Navy crest, from the airing cupboard. He then proceeded to pull a hair shirt from his rucsac but she frog-marched him through to the kitchen with orders to eat before thinking about penances.

The scones and homemade jam, plus strong hot tisane, soon cheered him up and the urge to wear the hair shirt receded. It, incidentally, was a going away present from his Mother to ward off naughty temptations which, in the present situation, Spike thought somewhat ironic!

She suggested, as they were leaving for Mass, that he turn his cloak inside out; 'Scarlet makes you stand out and we don't want you to stand out except for me!'

Spike replied that the observation was quite good for so early in the morning and had a good chuckle.

They retraced their steps along the path and she explained that Ole, the Mouse in Charge, would be on Mass Duty and he could have a word with him before the service. When they reached the side door Angelica took the lead and Spike followed close behind.

Ole

The backwall of the Cathedral, a spot selected by Ole's predecessor to oversee the mice during the Mass would, he swore to God, be the death of him. Umpteen pairs of socks and longjohns, plus all his faith and positive thinking, just saved him from a freezing death.

Angelica, with someone in tow, materialised out of the gloom and he waited in the shadows until they drew level then asked;

'Morning Angie, how's tricks. Is this one of them?'

As the someone moved from the shade into the light Ole recognised the cut of the other's cloak. The hand stitching along the front seam was the mark of Isaac Levymouse, the last of the traditional tailors working out of the Vatican Catacombs and no sailormouse would dare to wear one of his creations.

Switching quickly to the recommended ecclesiastical grovelling mode Ole apologised, mouse to mouse, for his thoughtless remark but said he hadn't received any staff notices regarding new arrivals. Angelica quietly took him to one side and whispered;

'He's sort of arrived with the Bishop as an unofficial travelling companion. I came across him wandering abroad, late last night, and took him under my wing.'

'Oh dear, oh dear, what a fate to befall any mouse wandering abroad let alone one from the Vatican!'

He gritted his teeth in pain as her heel found his instep.

'That's enough Angie. I just hope you weren't too inconvenienced.'

The following silence could only be described as pregnant, a common phrase around the Cathedral for that sort of silence, so Ole quickly returned to the business in hand;

'O'Rourke has failed to show up for duty and when he graces us with his presence he doesn't stay very long. With yesterday being pay-day could I have expected otherwise?'

Her companion, who hadn't uttered a word so far, confirmed that his social diary indicated a free day so where and when did Ole want him to start.

Spike

He selected a baghook from the rack and slipped it over his head feeling that his gainful employment more than compensated for a penance in the shape of a hair shirt. The job entailed picking up all the rubbish dropped during the service and he noticed also the easing off of a few boots and shoes. People's feet had always interested him and some of his associates would purposely swop shoes around but Spike had always adhered to the principal of *Get em up and get em out* in the fastest time to give the maximum break.

Working his way slowly towards the front he felt the urge to whistle but restrained himself and concentrated on the job in hand. Bits of fruit, apple cores, crusts of bread and a disgusting thing that shouldn't have been in a church in the first place, all ended up in the bag. Even a potential fire of smouldering pipe ash was doused before it could take hold.

His thoughts turned to home where, time back-a-long, he had learnt the rudiments of chess from Uncle Zeb. One lesson stuck in his mind above all others where, at the first move, a pawn is sacrificed in return for the probability of a piece of greater value.

It was called an *Opening Gambit* and Spike felt this an apt title for his move from home comforts to his present situation. Circumstances, some beyond his earthly control, had led this far with the next change of direction not too far away.

Angelica then came to mind and he recalled previous relationships, mainly with mouse nuns, which had always been problematic. However the housekeepers of Senior Churchmice were always most obliging to the younger set so hopefully it was the same in this area.

He had reached the front altar where he knelt, in a private silent prayer of thanks to St Christopher, and remembered his family and friends. As he stood and turned back to his duties a damson stone skimmed past his ear and a rough looking character materialised out of the gloom, said something that he didn't quite catch, shook him by the hand and melted back into the gloom.

Spike thought he was wearing some sort of tatty skirt but how was he expected to recognise a kilt in that light?

The weight of the bag was hurting his neck by the time the Mass ended so he unhooked it and returned to the bag-drop where Ole waited to introduce him to the others;

Gerard Du, the exchange mouse mentioned by Angelica, had an extraordinary long nose and was on a six-month sabbatical from Chartres.

MacDowell, the one in the kilt, hailed from Glasgow.

O'Rourke had arrived looking like he had just fallen out of a tree and could only manage a curt nod in Spike's direction.

Last of all was *Reggie*, a very shiny black mouse, on permanent loan from Balham Cathedral, who helped Spike load his bag on to the handcart.

'That's everyone so let's go and see what our Angie has cooked up for us.'

Her knees went wobbly when she looked up from her cheesecutting duties and spied Spike trailing in behind the rest. The cheese seemed crumbly this morning leaving her feeling the same, crumbly, as her golden rule about *not going* with the mice one works with was in tatters. Her mind was all of a dither but she knew the Lord would forgive this one indiscretion as the mouse in question was rather dishy.

Reggie's beaming face appeared at the counter to ask what was in the pots; 'Blackcurrant tisane and organically grown Cheese Rarebit for nibbles.'

He became even beamier as he poured the blackcurrent into his pot and, helping himself to the largest piece of Rarebit, remarked;

'Angie, Angie, where have you been all my life, what an occasion.'

Angelica eyeballed each one as they filed past the counter then, as she brought the new '*Thank you for not smoking*' signs to their attention, the puffers whiskers drooped and they muttered dark threats all the way to the tables.

Some of the customers had previously argued that it was their God given ancient right to send their prayers, encased in smoke, up to heaven but she was adamant as the fume-laden atmosphere had set off the innocent others wheezing and groaning.

Trouble may well have eventually erupted but Angelica pre-empted this by ordering the puffers to sit outside. Here the fumes would have an unrestricted path, straight up, and the puffers could cough and splutter to their hearts' content.

'And if I see any of you blowing your waccy-baccy in here then it will be an occasion believe me. I haven't spent all morning hanging these up for them to be ignored by you lot.'

Ole settled into a corner, bit into the toast, and gave an appreciative munch.

'So tell me your life story,' he asked Spike who obliged with a shortened version of events so far and the Mouse-in-Charge listened quietly before finishing his toast and draining his pot. 'I have your rucsac so let's say you spent the night in the kitchens as we have to protect both your reputations. Angelica was saddled with the most appalling debts after her parents business went bottoms up so what she does is one way to pay off the Augustine moneylenders. I am fond of her though and she is a good worker.'

He blew his nose on a very large handkerchief.

'At the moment we have our full staff quota but with O'Rourke I have the gravest concern. He is selling his blood to the alchemist for plague research, then using the money to buy drink, so I might be forced to restrain him in case something nasty surfaces.'

Ole paused and looked at Spike with some sadness before continuing;

'So I can only offer you on call casual work. The Almonermouse will pay you weekly and there is a spare cell in the block which we can sort out at the end of the shift.'

He stood and hooked the pot onto his belt before remarking, for Spike's benefit;

'I will mention to Angie about this toast, if anyone gets two bits it's me, not you!'

His departure signalled that the next Mass was about to commence so they all followed him back to the porch. MacDowell was sent away to change his kilt after Ole deemed it only fit to clean the kitchen floor and, as O'Rourke had disappeared yet again, Spike continued until the last service of the day working the same aisle.

A well-practised eye was passed over the floor. Ole then gave the thumbs up and the rest of the mice waved goodnight and headed off to bed leaving just the two of them to snuff out the candles and lock the doors.

In the past, according to Ole, the Cathedral had been left open but these days, even though a fliegermaus flight might be in residence, the structures were starting to crumble so the place had to be kept locked at night.

Spike looked around and remarked that the structures looked in good condition.

'The moral structure, not the fabric, the moral,' came the terse reply.

He wanted to ask about the fliegermaus. Uncle Zeb had shown him drawings and indicated a frightening shape flying overhead one dark night but he had never actually seen one close up. Ole looked very tired however so Spike shouldered his rucsac and followed him through the cloisters, into the library and along the internal panelling.

At the bottom of some steps the monastic cells, set in the stone structure, came into view and they reminded him of the punishment cells in the Vatican Catacombs. It was not until Ole lit a candle that he could see how clean and comfortable they were.

'This is yours for the moment,' said Ole, 'and down the corridor is the lavatorium, the raredorter behind and opposite is the calefactorium where you will find soap and pegs in the cupboard. Angie has put the general grab bag in your room, something might fit.'

He walked towards the door, paused and turned.

'Sleep well and, I meant to mention it before; I do like your pink socks!'

The bunk looked so inviting, all ready to leap on and snuggle down, but he opened the grab bag and found an old patched *Cistercian Order of Illustrious Monkmice* mouserobe that would suffice. He removed his boots, sorted through the clothes that had to be washed for tomorrow, and took the lot down to the lavatarium to soak whilst he treated himself to a good shower, a whisker shampoo and a brisk rubdown with a hair towel.

The final task was to hang his clothes in the calfactarium before returning to the cell. Family, friends were remembered and he looked around the drab walls to wonder which colour scheme might brighten up the place.

He imagined soft creamy beiges blending hot orange accents and a pair of vibrant graphics over the door as he climbed up onto the bunk and he was asleep before his head hit the pillow.

A cup of hot tisane started each working day that ended in the canteen with an evening meal and general socialising. Ole worked him with the rest of the churchmice which gave an opportunity to get to know them, together with their duties, around and within the Cathedral. Reggie had an allotment behind the gardener's shed growing something involving the *final pain*, Gerard designed and imported his own brand of handkerchiefs known locally as *Size 13s*, while a team of CathCats, smartly outfitted in white boots, gloves and hats, were responsible for the Cathedral security.

The CathCats duties normally consisted of Main Gate guard, and wandering pickets, but their present work load included the supervision of the plague footbath and any person, cat, rat or mouse sneaking past, without first soaking their footwear, were dealt with in a very severe manner. Mr Knyght, the keeper and player of the organ, who had somehow landed the duty of controller of cats, supplied an escort cat for the staff on request. Some areas of the town were deemed positively dangerous as the local vermin had no respect for the clothe or the wearer.

Spike had been instructed in all the basic church-mousing duties whilst at St Angelo's but had missed out on further tuition. Each morning he repeated the family motto of *'Above all-never stand on trifles'* and took every opportunity to learn and observe his allotted tasks.

MacDowell

His name was quickly marked opposite all the difficult jobs on Ole's work list simply because he was the most reliable member of the team.

'There's something nasty in the woodshed, send for MacDowell.'

'A corpse is rotting and needs to be moved, send for MacDowell.'

He was faced with a most unsavoury task one morning when the first group of visitors happened to be lepers from the Alms Hospital of the City. They descended on the Cathedral, en masse, to worship at the Shrine of St Osmond for the annual healing ceremony and a problem arose when the duty cat found a shoe left behind in the footbath following their arrival.

It contained a still twitching foot so the Controller of Cats was duly informed.

Mr Knyght hurried to the Shrine only to discover that the healing ceremony had already commenced with groups of lepers poking their diseased limbs into the various orifices of St Osmond's tomb. He carried on to the footbath where Ole, already on the job, looked up from the gruesome task of examining the foot to remark;

'We will deal with it Mr Knyght.'

MacDowell happened to walk past at that very moment and somehow got roped in. An innocent bystander one might say.

'Oh MacDowell! Collect what we need from the stores and meet me at the Shrine. And bring that new mouse with you, he needs the experience.'

No one seemed to care whether he was on duty or off and it was just assumed these orders would be followed.

'A problem has arisen and MacDowell will fix it'.

At the cells he changed into his working cloak and went to find Spike who was resting comfortably on his bunk after an early morning start. MacDowell explained the job, rather too graphically for Spike's delicate nature, on their way to the stores to collect the essentials before carrying on to the Shrine where the ceremony was just ending. The lepers moved off as a group so the aisles were quickly roped off as a few touristmice, some from foreign lands with their eyes on the slant, were starting to crowd around and gawp.

Ole lit a candle and circled around the tomb peering into the gloom of each orifice in turn. He remarked that there were not as many as last year, then helped the pair fit their masks and gloves, and watched as they dropped down onto the tomb floor. MacDowell didn't just sweep up the discarded segments into a pile but, as a sign of respect, gave a flourish each time before rolling them on to the dustpan and into the bag.

His actions seemed to impress the crowd who gave a few *ahs* and *ohs*. Spike said he felt quite ill so

MacDowell tried to take his mind off the job by pointing out the more unusual features of the pieces until Ole looked over and said;

'All finished then lads, just drop some killpong along the edges and call it a day.'

They put their disposables into the bag and Ole approached with his board to confirm a tally of nineteen pieces in all which included one and a half ears and a full nose. The details would be posted on the *Lost and Found* notice but Ole said he didn't hold much hope as last year's lot was still waiting to be claimed!

Reggie

There were a very few in for early Mass so the duty mice were soon in the canteen for toast, gruel and tisane. Reggie took doubles on everything and walked over to the far corner. Angelica appeared as Spike was filling his pot and, although they had met several times since that night, this was the first time alone.

'Lordy me, it's the wanderer abroad. How are you my dear?' she asked cheerfully in her early morning voice.

'Overworked, oversexed, and overhere.'

Spike couldn't believe that reply had come out of his own mouth and tried to keep a straight face. Angelica tried also to look appropriately shocked but they both failed on both counts and had a good chuckle instead.

'It must be the company you are keeping, but I am glad it's going right for you and we must meet again soon.'

'What are you growing behind the gardener's shed?' Spike asked when they were seated comfortably back at the table.

'Well man it's the old hash...' Reggie waited for a reaction but there were none.

'My grandfather brought seeds from the dark continent to plant in his allotment at Balham. Some survived but he said it was like smoking dried shit so I brought a few of the dormant seeds from home and planted them behind the gardener's shed.'

He chuckled and bit into his toast. 'It's like a corner of heaven. Warm, peaceful and hassle free and man, they thrived. They thrive man, so much so that if I didn't top them on a regular basis they would reach the steeple-cross.'

Another bite at his toast. 'And the smoke is sweet like Nookies Knocker.'

Spike tried to look as if he knew Nookies Knocker but had no idea really.

Reggie confirmed that *Mousestafarian Fine Cut* was smoked in all the best joints in town and the profits used to bury the plague victims. 'But I need to cultivate more to satisfy the demand as the dying, who need a toke in their last few hours, miss out.'

Spike's other question, about the *final pain*, had been answered.

They left the canteen to continue emptying the waste bins that were then loaded on to the cart. Reggie pulled while Spike pushed until they arrived behind the gardener's shed where wisps of smoke still rose from yesterday's burn-up.

The plantation grew behind a wattle fence and they checked for any snoopers before walking up to the gate. Reggie undid some thonging and stepped into the enclosure with Spike following who felt the warmth from the straw soaking through the soles of his boots.

Reggie explained that the patch, enclosed by three fences, had the south facing side lower than the others to take advantage of the sun's path. The area had been excavated with underfloor mudbrick ducting constructed so the warmth from the outside fire could travel along the ducts in a loop before returning to the source and into the air.

Clay troughs enclosed the plants that were set in rows and snuggled down in straw laid on top of the bricks to retain the heat. Chaff bales were then stacked up around the wattle fencing to complete that, which Reggie so rightly called, a little bit of heaven.

Spike thought the layout most ingenious.

He sat on a bench, in the winter's sun, to survey the situation and clear his thoughts with a few sweet blows from one of *Reggie's Rollups*. He heard of the low yield crops constantly reducing supplies and Ole's answer to that problem was to plant more seeds. Spike said he would definitely speak to Ole and the pair finally settled down to enjoy the rest of their smoke in an atmosphere of companionable silence.

A meeting was arranged and Spike sat in the office reading a large sign that said *Do not disturb this conference*. Eventually his boss arrived and, after only a few moments into the discussion, he could sense the frustration that Reggie must have felt.

Ole thought that the hash should be treated like any other vegetable and Spike listened patiently for a while, diplomousically, before trying to put his own point of view.

He couldn't get a word in edgeways so, at the first pause when Ole drew breath, he told his boss that they were wasting each other's time and stood up to leave. He was then told, in no uncertain manner, to sit down and explain the facts clearly and precisely.

Which he did and finished off by saying that hash needed to be nurtured and not just planted out and left like turnips. Ole said nothing so Spike carried on.

'To extend the patch would take extensive excavations requiring waste from the outside to keep the larger fires going and this would draw the attention of the authorities. Any other area would have to be within walking distance with its own drying patch away from prying eyes. Reggie has it very well organised, if I may say so, but on a smaller scale.'

Ole rolled his eyes and told him to get to the point.

'We can ask the Mouse in Charge at St Thomas' if we can use their graveyard or try to increase our present yield by intensive cultivation.'

'St Thomas' yard is out of the question', replied Ole, and then asked how the yield could be increased. Spike replied that his Uncle Zeb, who'd had a great deal of experience in that sort of thing, could be reached by m-mail asking for advice. The meeting was thereby concluded and they walked over to the canteen for a well-earned lunch.

Epistle Three

Ole

A parcel had arrived at the Cathedral earlier in the week to disappear into Ole's private *to be kept locked at all times* cupboard. It had clear markings in Vaticanese that included Giovanni's name and the address.

An application for a work permit had already been sent off so Spike, in theory, had yet to arrive. Ole decided to put the package to one side in case the authorities enquired into this unlisted work permit-less mouse by the name of Giovanni. If they had then he would have written *'Not known at this address'* and returned the parcel to them.

The postmouse who knew most tongues delivered the parcel and translated the script from Latin to English. It read;

'Do not open until my lovely boy Giovanni's birthday being spent so far away from his family and friends. The apple of his Mother's eye doing such fine work in England with his Eminence the Cardinal, another of our fine boys of whom any Mother would be so proud if she had been alive, which she isn't just now you know. God rest her soul.'

At that point the postmouse lost the thread of the script as, to quote his words;

'This Mothermouse goes on and on…'

He charged a standard translation half groat and continued with his round.

The parcel was produced with an ecclesiastical flourish when Spike arrived at the office to collect it and Ole explained why it had been kept in the cupboard.

'Mother must have got the address from Uncle Zeb's m-mail,' he explained and a wet-eye started before he'd even finished undoing the outer wrapper. A good nose blow, into one of Gerard's size 13s, made him feel better and the smell of home wafted up from a box containing several presents of various sizes and shapes. He selected the largest and, opening it up, pulled out a large piece of silk fixed together with some cord.

It lay between them as Spike translated the label;

'The Leonardo da Vinci Parachute Company. We stand by our name and give a full refund if any of the products fail in service. Full instructions on the back of this label.'

He turned the label over. *'Secure the straps of the parachute over your shoulders and tuck the canopy, lightly folded, under the left arm. Climb to a high place and make sure there is no one below you or anything pointy sticking up which could impale you.*

Take a deep breath before jumping up and forward with a positive attitude and fling the canopy upwards You will float safely to earth without breaking your arm, leg or head.'

It ended with. *'Happy Birthday Son, Love Mum XXX.'*

Ole found it difficult to keep a straight face and wondered, aloud unfortunately, whether that was the correct translation of the label.

'Of course it is,' replied Spike quite sharply, 'I do read the language you know.'

Ole then tried, albeit unsuccessfully, to stifle his laughter after that sharp retort, with the situation made worse by the serious expression on Spike's face.

'God almighty, you don't believe that crap and expect to survive?'

Spike handed him a spare size 13 and waited until he'd regained his composure before answering;

'Leonardo was our greatest engineering inventor and Uncle Zeb, who was doing holiday relief at the Medici Chapel in San Lorenzo, saw some of the parachute sketches which Michelangelo had in his folder.'

Ole replied that he thought da Vinci had invented it.

'He did, he did,' answered Spike stuffing the parachute back in its wrapper, 'and Michelangelo admired his work so much but I didn't know they were in production.'

He picked up the parcel and opened the door to leave but paused then asked;

'If I told you that my Grandmother sat for Leonardo da Vinci when he was painting the 'Mona Lisa', for the reason that no human could be found with such haunting eyes, would you believe me?'

'Obviously not,' thought Spike judging by the expression on Ole's face so he thanked him and walked in the direction of the accommodation where he could examine the rest of his parcel in the privacy of his own cell.

Anonymouse, Early November 1528

The midweek early Mass during the winter months normally attracted only the most pious of clergy and laymen. The Vatican's social and financial calendars were in tatters so no longer could the canons, leaving England's fog and ecclesiastical duties to their subordinates, swan off to the Italian Riviera where the living was easy.

Vin ordinaire [local plonk] and Mudeford caviare [local sardines] appeared on the canons' lunch menus instead of the usual Vin superiere and Caspian caviare which confirmed a definite drop in their living standards and they felt obliged to attend the services which, after all, were part of their chosen profession.

The Chapter Wine Cellar, situated beneath the Bishop's Palace, had been established over the decades to be admired but solely by word of mouth or hear of ear. When asked why only a select few had access to the area, The Cellarer cited a higher authority but it was the phenomenon known as *Stock Control* that he had never quite got to grips with.

The Bishop only visited on rare occasions but when he did he always brought plenty of *Duty Free* items in his luggage and this led to lots of quality wine coming into the cellar and very little going out. This absence of stock control however would have caused no problems if the Cellarer had only shaken his working habit upside down on that particular day before giving it to the Chamberlain. He, in turn, took it down to the washhouse for a rub-a-dub with the cellar keys still in the pocket.

The laundryman on duty, a dubious character by the name of Potts, found the items and quickly made a soap impression. He was always on the look-out for a quick groat and knew that keys, especially those belonging to high officials, had value.

Soon the Cellarer himself came down the steps in search of the lost items and Potts held them out. 'Just wiping them dry my Lord; I caught them as they disappeared down the hole.' They were snatched away, without a word of thanks, but the Cellarer proffered his ring to be kissed before leaving the washhouse without further ado.

Potts wrapped the soap in a piece of oilcloth and remembered that clean aprons, for the stained glass workshops, were due to be delivered that afternoon. Several windows were being worked on at the time so Potts took this opportunity to ask a favour from a friend of his who assisted the glaziers with the leadwork. Soft metal casts of the keys were soon safely in the hands of the laundryman and that evening, by the light of a single candle, he made iron copies of the keys and pondered where they fitted.

For the Cellarer himself to fetch them they must be very important!

A laundryman's job included the delivery and collection of clean and soiled articles and one such call was to the Bishop's Palace basement linen store where Potts noticed that the lockplate had a design etching similar to the keys he had copied.

And the same pattern was duplicated on the wine cellar lockplate next door.

Possession of an unlawful key would mean mega-time in the stocks but Potts, covering his actions by moving the cart, took the keys from his apron pocket and tried the first one. The door moved open so he quickly shut and locked it again.

'Praise the Lord,' he rejoiced quietly, 'the key to the Bishop's wine cellar.'

He moved away to consider a situation that had to be handled very carefully. Filching a few bottles for his own use would be no problem but a higher being could utilise this opportunity to bring greater rewards for both parties.

Someone in authority who was obviously bent.

He knew just such a person!

A plan of action had to be mapped out with his share of the profits guaranteed but until that happened he could not keep the keys or leave them lying around. They would have to be hidden in a safe place.

He knew just the place!

Spike, Below the Chantry

Resting peacefully on his bunk, after an early morning start, he was rudely awoken by something noisy being pushed into the vent shaft of the cell. Bits of daub fell on his head so he jumped on to the floor and hurried to the lavatarium where, by standing on the bath ledge, he could look along the outside wall. A discreet cough and Gerard, waiting to have a shower, climbed up beside him and all they could see was the laundry cart but then a man came into view and started to push the cart away.

Gerard identified the departing figure as Potts the laundryman.

They got down from the ledge and returned to the cell where Spike lit a candle and explained what had happened. Gerard, being the taller, removed the grill and managed to get his head in the vent but was unable to make out what was stuck up there. He then stood on a box, putting head and hands up the vent, and after a lot of coughing, sneezing and some *Mon Dieus*, pronounced the verdict that it was a pair of keys, mansize not mousesize!

Stepping down he stood, all dusty and cobwebby, then gave his nose a hard long blow into one of his own size 13 handkerchiefs especially made to fit size 13 noses. 'My nose tells me there is something in the wind,' he confirmed when he'd finished.

'I'll have my shower while you go and find the boss.'

Spike swept up the mess and then fetched Ole, who had just arrived at the office, and reiterated the events as they walked over to the Chantry's outer walls.

A leather strip looped out from the vent but Ole didn't want to hang around staring so they returned inside where Gerard kept muttering about a high quality mouse taking charge.

He was asked to clarify the statement.

'We of the French Clothe have an uncanny knack of sniffing out wrong doings and I'd like to resolve the mystery of Monsieur Potts' keys but I must be in charge from the very beginning.'

'God you are a pain in the butt. Are all Frenchmice like you?'

This remark caused a typically French splutter.

Ole continued. 'All right Gerald, stop spluttering, but everything has to be off the record so keep me informed and don't tread on any toes.'

He then stood up and asked Spike to give the French mouse a hand for the rest of the day.

For some time Gerard continued to splutter and mutter that all these dreadful slurs cast upon the Churchmice of France would be noted in his Gallican Diary and he, in time, would demand an apology from Ole. He kept on and on about the *Churchmice Superiore of the French Clothe* before finally getting down to the task in hand.

The keys were too valuable for Potts to keep on his person, hence the hidey-hole, and they would be collected when needed. Limited mousepower only was available so any alarm system had to be fully automatic with its sole requirement being that someone had to be within earshot of the cell. A leather thong was first looped up through the keyring and down again with the ends tied to a selected stone poised above an iron bucket. When the keys were pulled out of the vent the leather would break and the pieces, together with the stone, would fall into the bucket. No evidence would be obvious that the keys were tied to anything, so the key puller-outer would think he had just dislodged something in the vent.

The breaking strain of the leather was slightly higher than the mass of the stone and this was worked out with quill, ink and parchment on the floor of the cell to a secret formula known only to the French Clothe. Gerard sent Spike out during the final calculations so he started to move his gear into the other spare cell. It was late by the time they finished and Gerard unexpectedly thanked him for his help but reverted to typical *Frenchmouse Form* with the remark that he seemed unusually bright for an Italian!

Spike felt like making a comment about his nose but it would have gone over his head, the comment not the nose, so he went to the washroom and washed his hands ready for the evening meal. The rest of the churchmice were then told of the plan and Ole ordered a cell watch list to be drawn up. This would ensure that someone would always be around to hear the clatter of the stone falling into bucket.

Angelica, Mid November 1528

She rinsed out her cloth into the pail while considering her immediate prospects. They did not look at all good and tears fell onto the lavatorium floor that she was endeavouring to clean on that cold and wet Saturday afternoon. The Augustine moneylenders would soon be around to collect their weekly dues which, at this point in time, were conspicuously absent from her purse.

The wool barges, trapped up river at Wilton by the floodwater, had been delayed for some time so there were no free-spending sailormice in town and, although she planned a stroll around the centre that evening, the idea depressed her as the area crawled with all sorts of weirdos. However an almighty crash then resounded from one of the corridors so that train of thought was abruptly terminated.

'Lordy, lordy me, what on earth was that?' she said to no one in particular and rushed towards the noise where the sound of heavy footsteps, sloshing through puddles and moving quickly away in the distance, could be heard above the pouring rain.

And on the floor of the cell were the upturned bucket, the stone and the piece of leather all lying together in a distressed condition.

'God in heaven, God in heaven.' The phrase was repeated as she realised that O'Rourke, the duty mouse, had disappeared at lunchtime on one of his drinking sprees and hadn't returned.

It momentarily crossed her mind to put on something decent but there was no time so out the door she tumbled into the pouring rain. With her feet in a fast shuffle mode, and wearing only her pinny, curlers and scuffs, she followed the keys with a trademark look of grim determination on her face that was a true reflection of the English fighting spirit.

The CathCat was not around either when she reached the Main Gate and, although the footbath and the surrounds were flooded, whoever was rostered for duty should have been on hand for this was the one time when their help would have been greatly appreciated.

Through the Gate and along the High Street she tracked the cloaked figure, acutely aware that she looked a dreadful sight with her hair all bedraggled, one scuff lost down the drain and her mouse maid's knee giving her hell, but she bravely kept the target in view until it arrived at the gate of St Thomas'

Church. Angelica paused as this was the rough end of town and the surrounding area had a very bad reputation—it was positively dangerous.

The figure waited a moment then walked up the path to the church door and rang the bell. It was quickly answered and one of the vicars, a tall stooping man whom she vaguely recognised, snatched the package.

A movement behind the stones alerted her so she quickly tried to retrace her steps but the gang leader's voice broke the silence of the rain a short distance from the gate.

'Look what we have here then lads, the tart from the Cathedral if I'm not mistaken. Sent down to spy on us no doubt so let's have a welcoming party for her.'

Many hands dragged her into the grass as she fought and struggled but her efforts were in vain. She was thrown off balance against a gravestone and the subsequent knock on the head, mercifully, caused her to lose consciousness.

Trouble flared that evening in the canteen when the supper was late being served. Angelica, responsible for the food preparation, couldn't be found anywhere in the area prompting a scale two alert within the Close. A fracas then started around the same time in the cells when the mice, returning from their respective jobs tired and soaking wet, spotted the upturned bucket which indicated the keys had been removed.

Curses of *Mon Dieus* and *Dear God* filled the air.

Gerard accused MacDowell of being absent from duty, after mistakenly looking at next week's duty rota, while the Glaswegian threatened, and was about to proceed, to detach Gerard's head from the rest of his body. Ole arrived in time to calm the situation and to escort a violently simmering Scotsmouse to a supper that eventually materialised but was uneatable.

Angelica had prepared the meal but failed to light the faggots under the pot before finishing her shift. Her relief, who happened to be Ole's niece, arrived to find the fire unlit and the meal uncooked. Prudence tried to rectify the situation by immediately lighting the fire but turnip vindaloo needs a lot of cooking and half cooked is worse than not cooked. So the absence of any eatable supper triggered a red alert in the stomachs of the hungry mice.

Ole and Prudence checked her room to no avail and continued on to the work area. She was a conscientious worker who would tidy up and put things away so this fact, added to the upturned bucket and a half cleaned floor in the lavatorium, indicated that something, or someone, must have interrupted her. This gave cause for the gravest concern and when Gerard returned, to confirm that the keys had gone, the rest of the staff quickly assembled to move into Spike's cell where Ole opened up the proceedings.

'We have to assume that Angie was here on her own when the keys were taken so it looks as if she followed the key puller. Any other ideas?'

MacDowell, glaring pointedly at Gerard, asked about O'Rourke and was assured that his absence would be severely dealt with. It was suggested that the Duty CathCat might have seen her at the Main

Gate so the rest started a local ground search while Ole paid a visit to the Bell Tower Compound to check with the Three Cs.

Old Harry was the Cathedral Cat in Charge with whom he had worked for a number of years and they were both due to retire shortly. On arrival at his house Ole wondered if Harry was suffering from Diogenes Syndrome as he waded through the piles of rubbish that littered the garden path to finally reach the back door.

A few sharp raps seemed to echo through the house so he pushed the door open to find the inside a worse tip than the garden. Harry then appeared around the corner, his arms full of bottles of home brew, to suggest they share one but Ole confirmed that this was no social call and related recent events before asking if any of the CathCats were missing.

'Not to my knowledge,' was the reply but he went off to double check and Ole sat down to wait on the garden seat. The cat soon returned to relate that a new member on a job experience scheme, a relation of Noah the Dean's cat, had let the team down badly.

The bile rose in Ole's throat as he struggled to give the appearance of being in control. What did the cat actually mean by the phrase *let the team down*?

Harry seemed to take an avid interest in the floor as he spoke;

'Tibbles didn't think it necessary to keep gate watch when he was getting soaked through in the heavy rain so he went home.'

At that point it all became too much and Ole let rip.

'Do you mean to say that one of my staff could be

in the gravest danger because your Tibbles was frightened of getting bloody wet?'

Harry told him to keep his hairshirt on and turned to go.

'I haven't finished yet. Is this Tibbles that thing with the orange streak in his hair and a ring through its nose, one of the New Breed?'

Ole then concluded in a tone that sent shivers down Old Harry's spine;

'If our Angie is hurt in any way then you tell him that his nosering will be personally ripped off and his scrawny neck threaded through it.'

Ole does try, really tries, as he's on ragwort balm for high blood pressure, and any serious upset gives him heartburn for days with the Cathedral routine going all to pot.

The cat tried to leave again but was called back.

'Get your team here double quick. I want them in full riot gear with batons and chains and we'll go through this town like a dose of salts until we find her. This sort of slack behaviour really gets my goat and I want them all here including, and especially, your Tib, Tib, Tib. I can't even say the bloody name but bring that cat, do you understand?'

Harry hurried away in standard ecclesiastical shuffling mode muttering about Mr Knyght and confirmation but the cat knew full well that Ole had the authority to act as he saw fit depending on the circumstances of the moment.

And he was acting as he saw fit at that moment!

Bringing the staff up to date seemed to calm him down as he confirmed that Angelica must have followed the target outside the gate so God only knows where she could be now.

'I want one team to search along the river bank, another one up the High Street and the last one to circle around the Bishop's Palace. All teams meet at St Thomas' where I will be waiting with Old Harry.'

Gerard raised an arm to speak and Ole nodded.

'Angie might well have followed and saw the keys passed over but us acting like the Vandals could warn the guilty party off. Let's try softly softly until we find her and then, if we need force, the heavy mob can handle it.'

The meeting waited for Ole's reply;

'He's right you know, Angie's work could be wasted. Get the cats out of their uniforms, into mufti, but may I suggest they take a few hidden persuaders just in case.'

MacDowell teamed up with a cat called Bruno who was on holiday relief from Christchurch Priory. He supplied the brawn while the mouse supplied the local knowledge and together they took the river route. Reggie and Gerard, with a real scrapper of an ex-naval cat called Erskine, took the back gate route. The two remaining cats, Scrimshaw and Spindrift, patrolled the Main Gate whilst keeping a good eye out in case they were needed. Ole had christened them the heavy mob to be called out in times of strife.

The rest took to the High Street.

Spike walked with *That Cat*, as Ole called him, and felt sorry for him to be saddled with a name like Tibbles so it was shortened to TC. A shoe, that turned out to be one of Angelica's scuffs, was then spotted floating in the High Street ditch amongst the sewage.

The job of fishing it out was designated to TC!

As they examined the shoe Ole thought he saw a flashing light in the tower of St Thomas' church and wondered aloud if it was meant for them. While waiting for further signals he explained that the Incumbents of St Thomas' had evacuated the church when a vicar contracted the plague. A bent Chapter Curate, by the name of Obadiah Lopes who had very nearly lost his calling regarding some missing silver plate, had offered to stand in as Church Warden.

But he'd soon gambled away all the money given by the parish to maintain the Cats so they left and the Graveyard Gang moved in leading to a break-down in law and order. Norman was the Mouse in Charge and had been bailed up inside the Church for a number of weeks now.

Ole stopped talking to concentrate when the light started another flashing sequence.

'It's signalling Midland Mousecode and they need to talk, let's see what they want.'

Old Harry immediately volunteered to go into the church on his own as, he remarked, it might look suspicious if they all went.

'Hangfire for a moment,' warned Ole. 'A head of security passing unguarded through the graveyard will be dangerous. You aren't young any more so it might be best if Spike and TC go by themselves. They are strangers in the area and could be taking a short cut to the market.'

And the closing statement that they could run a damn sight faster started TC off crying. His tears ran along his whiskers to drip on the ground causing Old Harry to remark;

'Now look what you've done. The thought of violence scares Tibbles stiff and once he starts it takes hours for him to stop.'

The cat's performance was attracting attention so Ole walked up and dragged TC's nose ring very close. 'Listen deadhead,' he whispered but loud enough. 'You go with Spike or else I'll personally thread your thick head back through this ring. Make your choice.'

Spike felt it in his best interest to keep quiet at this point so he did!

TC's eyes blinked away the tears and his teeth chattered in unison with the clattering of their boots as the pair walked briskly towards the church. The door opened slightly on their approach and a voice ordered them inside; 'Quickly, quickly.'

They squeezed by the door and the voice continued in nervous staccatoed bursts;

'My name is Norman, the Mic. Forgive my manners as everything seems to be happening today and our lookout will give a call when Lopes is spotted. You must then leave at once as he is a most odious man who can smell strangers a long way off. We have Angelica who is a very sick mouse so follow me.'

At the back of the church and through a side door they found her sitting in front of the kitchen fire, wrapped in a blanket, and being fed from a bowl by a mouse introduced as Luke. With one eye shut and bleeding, a piece missing from an ear and the side of her lovely whiskers ripped, she looked a picture of dejection.

Her broken tooth did not make the picture any happier and their look of shock made her reach out and burst into tears. Spike's compassion turned to apprehension as her sobbing receded into a snuffling silence and he held her tightly until she slumped forward into his arms.

Norman laid her gently back in the chair.

'We cannot provide the proper medical treatment, she keeps drifting in and out of consciousness so help is urgently needed.'

Spike asked what on earth had happened and was told that Luke had found her at the back door, dumped on top of the garbage, with the rain pouring down. They had managed to keep her warm and brought her inside once Lopes was out of the way and then Ole was sighted in the High Street where the signal contact was made.

The lookout called loudly from above and Norman insisted that Angelica be moved. There was no time to discuss anything with Ole so Spike had to act alone and at once.

'We'll have to fix her somehow to TC, maybe on his back.'

The cat was called over to lie flat by the fire but, feeling cold and fed up, he moved far too slow. Stamping on the cat's tail with his boot increased the speed threefold, a trick Spike had learnt in the Vatican to move slow cats, and TC was soon fully alert in the right position.

'Now we have to keep her from sliding off. If we tie her on the pain will be too much so what else can we do?'

Norman suggested they use goose fat and fetched a large lump of it from the larder. Angelica was then lifted, laid flat across the cat's back, and snuggled down in the fur.

A look of horror spread itself across TCs face as the fat was liberally applied but no complaint seemed forthcoming. They exited out the back door, in the direction indicated by Luke along the edge of the graveyard, and the rain continued to pour down.

On reaching the main path Spike paused. He heard the front gate bang and the Curate passed by them not a whisker's width away. The chink of the bottles they heard, the stagger in his walk they noted, and the smell of quality claret pervaded his person. He entered the church by kicking the door open so they waited a while before resuming their journey of mercy.

Spike again pulled TC's ear to stop and it was lucky he did as two CriminalMice from the Graveyard Gang staggered out in front of them, wielding swords, and one opened his mouth to speak. But only a death rattle emerged then they both fell forward, *lifus extinguished*, into the grass.

'You have found her, that's good. Chop chop, let's get the hell out of here now!'

Then Ole, together with MacDowell, quickly dragged the two neatly garrotted bodies off the main path and behind one of the gravestones.

The procession had all the joys of a funeral, minus the dirge, when it reached the Cathedral just before sunrise, and passed through the Main Gate on their way to the canteen to where the *MouseMedic Team* were waiting, in full standby mode, for the casualty to arrive.

The Aftermath at St Thomas'

Further revelations

Another week has passed so, as a break from the daily grind of narrating, I've looked at the bulkier of the four journals entitled; *'Stickman of the South Pacific My sketchbook; 1859–65.'*

There were copious drawings with footnotes and I wondered about the 'Soldier of Fortune and Layman of the Clothe' title. However, tucked in the back under the chart-paper dust cover, was an envelope addressed to someone in Chatham.

I carefully slid out and positioned the letter under the magnifying lamp. It was several pages thick and headed; 'The Cincinnati Missionary Society on Canton Island in the Phoenix Group'. Another Canton? – I consulted my atlas to find that Canton Island was the largest of the Group, quite near to the Gilbert and Ellis Islands in fact, so the name was a coincidence.

The last page bore the signature of Rev Aaron Buzacott Jnr, with the name 'Alsa Piringa' below it, and contained an account of the drowning of William Stickman and details of his burial, with full military honours, in the graveyard at Nikumaroro.

Evidently the safety clips on his folding Welsh Coracle, one that he frequently used for his inter-island trips, came undone as he entered the harbour in bad weather. He was unable to secure them and the coracle folded, with him enshrouded within, to quickly sink to the bottom of the lagoon. The natives dived, alas too late to save him, and they brought the body ashore in their 'Necrophiliacanoo' flying the Jack at half mast.

The writer confirmed that, although the deceased was not ordained, he was a lay preacher who was an expert in the restoration of chapel bells and steeple crosses and would be sorely missed. They delayed the burial for a few weeks as the body lacked an arm and local custom dictated that a body had to be interned complete or eaten.

However an American Whaler happened upon the scene and marooned one of their crew who was at death's door. The natives chopped off his arm before he died, local custom again which no doubt hastened his death, then sold the remains to Poxfam and William Stickman, together with the arm, was eventually laid to rest resplendent in his shroud of Welsh Coracle. The fact that the marauding party brought back the wrong arm was noticed by quite a few but the witchdoctor decreed that the overall appearance didn't look too bad at all!

The writer then gave a brief outline of the deceased's life so I'll come back to that a bit later on in the book.

Epistle Four

The Mending Begins

Ole's wife Margaret, known during her nursing years as *Sister Carbolic* had, with her niece Prudence, set up the kitchen as an emergency sick bay and a fire burned under a large pot of water while they awaited the patient.

It took some time to unstick Angelica from TCs back before transferring her to the wattle carrycot and this was then gently laid on the worktable. Many herbs and soothing potions were on hand and the churchmice were asked to leave so the job of mending Angelica could begin at once and everything mousingly possible would be done.

Margaret promised regular progress reports and, although she had never really approved of Angelica, the sight of the torn body covered in a gooey mess softened the most hardened hospital heart. She was cleaned, stitched, bandaged and soothed with extra care but their task was made more difficult by periods of extreme agitation that depleted her already low energy level and, after she was settled into a hospital cot, it became obvious that something special was needed to put her to sleep.

Spike recommended that Reggie be consulted on this problem with the result that a little of the *Mousestafarian Fine Cut* now smouldered in a bowl nearby.

Angelica awoke in a panic, even before she could benefit from the Fine Cut, to find herself tightly bound in swaddling wraps, from head to tail, and unable to talk, move or twitch a whisker.

Her friends returned and quietly observed as Ole approached the patient and dangled a bunch of keys in front of her. Margaret scolded him to leave but he loosened off Angelica's headband and put his mouth close to her ear.

'Did you follow the keys to St Thomas'?'

Her expression changed as she focused on the keys.

She remembered and nodded her head.

The mice conferred and decided that Lopes was the only person in St Thomas' as Norman hadn't mentioned any visitors.

Putting his mouth again close to her ear Ole asked;

'Did he give the keys to a tall man and receive anything in return?'

An affirmative nod was all he needed.

'Lopes must have the keys and, from his drunken behaviour, they might just be the ones from the Bishop's drinks cupboard or even the winecellar.'

Angelica then lost consciousness so plans for a watch pattern were discussed with a shift of two hours apiece decided upon. Reggie took the first watch and his fine-cut wafted around helping to calm the patient. Margaret and Prudence were on call if needed so Spike, who had drawn a later slot, started back to his cell for a shower and few hours shuteye.

TC was pacing up and down outside feeling very concerned so Spike assured him that all was being done and a good pray, before bed, might well help.

'I hope so but I've got to face Mother who'll go potty when she sees my coat and I'm hours late for my supper!'

Spike nodded sympathetically and, while walking slowly back, decided that, as far as cats go anyway, TC was O.K.

Spike

The Inauguration the Boy Bishop was usually held mid December but on this occassion it was brought forward two weeks and only the faithful few turned up for the early Mass.

Spike was leaning against the side door when another churchmouse, complete with bag and hook, came shuffling by. The figure came to a halt as a wizened head poked itself out from the mousecloak, said 'Howdy', and carried on shuffling.

Reggie later explained that the old mouse's name was Victor who cared for the bells and kept a headcount of any fliegermaus in residence. He spent most of his time high in the bell tower and only came down to earth for special occasions. Some staff members thought him rather odd as he related tales of strange designs, around harvest time, impressed into the surrounding cornfields. They were called *Corn Circles* and Victor, who had spent most of his time above the level of the mere mortalmice, kept a record of the patterns.

When the service ended Spike wanted to meet Victor but the old mouse had gone so the pair stopped over at the canteen to enquire after Angelica's progress. The patient was stable but Prudence, on duty and very stoned from the ambience of the smouldering hash, flung her arms around Spike's neck before declaring her undying love for him causing Reggie to remark that this crop must be of a very high quality indeed!

TC waited at the Main Gate and mournfully related the happenings of the previous week. He told of a Mother beside herself with rage, an afternoon spent in the bath being scrubbed with carbolic soap by an irate Father, no tea or supper and his pocket money stopped for one whole month. The cat said he had tried to explain but neither of them would listen.

Spike assured him that Ole would have a word on his behalf but spoke before thinking how the boss would react to that request!

They carried on down the High Street and discussed the morning's mission. The tower of St Thomas' was visible from the Cathedral Main Gate so, if a signal was transmitted from the tower whenever Lopes left the church, his movements could be monitored around the Close.

'So,' Spike confirmed, 'we have to contact the tower and explain this.'

The cat knew some catcode but, on hearing that the mouse was a retired seconder from the Vatican Mousecubs, the 3rd Holy Trinity Pack of Angels no less, he knew he was in the company of an expert mousecoder. TC lit the tallow lamp, handed it to Spike, who gave the signal mirror a good polish and flashed the tower. He waited then flashed again, and again, and again. It was not until the people started to file out of the church that Spike realised there had been a service going on and felt such a pillock.

Not just any service though but one for the Unrepentant Sinner which the Local Gentry felt obliged to attend!

It was an hour before they received a response, with only half the message being read before the lamp failed. It had run dry of tallow but Luke, on duty in the tower, had read enough to confirm the request after which the pair returned to the Cathedral.

On reaching the Main Gate they turned, on intuition, and were very nearly run down by Lopes striding towards them with the lamp from the tower winking frantically over his shoulder. They angled off from his obvious direction of travel, and watched as he skirted the eastern boundary to turn into the gateway of one of the houses, so they made a note of the number and then separated to enjoy their respective lunch breaks.

The crowds arrived early that afternoon for the Inauguration Parade with Auxiliary CathCats operating the shoe and boot wash while endeavouring to keep some semblance of order around the Main Gate. Some of the town ladies refused to dip their shoes into the filthy water but the cats were adamant despite something in the paw being frequently offered to look away!

'No dippy, no watchy'.

Spike went down to lend a hand but crowd control was not his forte and, as chaos reigned supreme, he left the cats to it.

Master Thomas Bennet, the Vicar General, stood in for the Cardinal and crowned the youngest chorister to be Bishop for the day. His powers were somewhat restricted compared with previous years but everyone seemed to enjoy the event.

Spike later saw Spindrift towing O'Rourke, whose head was shaved clean and whiskers cropped short, along at a rope's end on the rubbish detail. He would have spoken, and wanted to, but the prisoner's hands were shaking so badly that they could hardly hold the sack so Spike just nodded a cursory greeting.

Ole had put him under work punishment until *the moon turns to cheese*!

Arriving at the canteen Spike found the patient calm but both the attendants stoned by the hashsmoke. Margaret related the afternoon's happenings, between giggles, to explain that Prudence had always fancied Gerard Du and went on to say that the smoke had encouraged the young girlmouse to tell him so.

His reply was that the French Clothe did not mix with servant mice.

Margaret said she felt like clouting the long nosed stuck up prig before laughingly revealing that Prudence had then accused him of being *gay*.

'You know, Qweer.'

Spike confirmed that he knew what Qweer meant.

Margaret continued to say how Gerard had returned with Ole to make Prudence apologise. She complied by standing outside the canteen and yelling at the top of her voice:

'Gerard-Du of the French Clothe is not, I'm sorry to say, Qweer.'

This made Ole embarrassed and he pulled her back inside by her ear. She yelped so loudly that

Margaret first called her husband a great pillock before chasing Gerard with a yard brush whilst shouting that it was all his fault.

Spike thought a few sympathetic noises might do the trick.

They didn't and Margaret continued on saying that she didn't know what made young girlmice tick or understand how Prudence, an attractive well brought up young ladymouse, could fancy anything French but Gerard, they all agreed, should have handled it in a far more diplomatic way. The conversation ended in tears with Margaret wondering why she had called Ole a big pillock.

Spike said he thought it was a most appropriate expression for the moment and, as the innocent bystander, he promised to explain the effects of hash to her husband and maybe sort out the disagreement.

Goodbye kisses followed with Margaret's even including a little tongue!

It was early evening before he saw Ole to mention the different effects of hash who replied that Margaret had just had a funny turn. He went on to say that Lisa, the anchoress from Foulstone with her singing group, would be arriving to help out in the lead up to Xmas. Although their music didn't interfere with the work, he warned Spike to be on his guard as Lisa had a distinct appetite for new churchmice in town.

Spike picked up some writing gear before starting his shift as a letter home was long overdue and it had to catch the morning's post. On arrival at the canteen Margaret wished him happy birthday, something that had completely slipped his mind, and gave him an update on the patient, a quick peck but this time on the cheek, and left him to it.

As he looked at Angelica, snoring gently and peacefully in her cot, he remembered that the Augustine moneylenders would soon be calling for their dues. She was trying to settle her parent's horrific debts, by paying the interest off from her earnings, but she was in no position at the moment to pay anyone so he jotted down a note to remind Ole.

The ambience of the hashsmoke drifted around the room as the patient's breathing became more relaxed and Spike started the letter. His wordflow was set to wax almost poetical but he stuck to straightforward prose as Mother would pass it on to Aunt Hester. If he wrote in too flowery terms then she would tell everyone within mousearshot;

'The boy sounds like he's in with an arty-farty crowd.'

Reggie relieved him before ten o'clock and, after a patient update, he returned tired and weary to his cell. Sitting on the bunk he lit a candle before selecting, from one of his presents, a nut truffle and wished himself a very, very happy birthday.

TC was waiting to escort him up the High Street to where he could send an m-mail and post his letter. On the way Spike explained to the cat that his Uncle Zeb had served with the Chaplain's Corps in Northern Italy where he had met some Swiss Armymice Nurses.

They told of their overall boss, an Army Surgeon by the name of Bombastus Paracelsus who believed in the theory that what made a person ill could also cure if the body was prepared correctly. He then created a potion using a selection of Herbarium products, to a secret formula, for this natural healing process. 'Laudanum' was the name and Spike hoped that Uncle might have the recipe, plus the list of ingredients, of the potion.

If it worked well on humans then it should work on other species, such as their good selves, and Angelica would be in with a fighting chance.

How the m-mail worked no one seemed to know. In the centre of 'MinuteMouseEmporium' stood a tall box with a curly horn protruding from the top and a large green button with the words. 'Push to enter message.' On the side was a long handle with further instructions. 'Pull this lever when finished and don't forget to pay at the desk.'

Spike had used the machine before, to send his Uncle a query about the hash crop, but he didn't feel confident at all balanced on the chair. He eventually shouted however, loudly into the horn without any breaks, the m-mail address before carrying on with the message.

'unclezeb.castlestangelo@viadellaconcihazione. vaticancity.co'

'How can you mend a ladymouse who has a bad case of sarlice?

She is on 'chi lavora la canapa'. Love to Mum. Giovanni. XXX.

He pushed the button and counted to ten before pulling the handle. The machine shook violently and gave a strangulated gurgle causing Brian, the manager, to make a comment that he really must get the servicemice in from Exxox to look at it. Spike then handed over the letter and asked for a bill for the m-mail as the costs could be claimed back from *The Hospital Plan Insurance*.

Brian promised to contact Spike immediately a reply came through and asked that his best wishes be passed on to Angelica.

Anonymouse

Two large black canonmice advanced towards him as Spike passed through the Main Gate and he waited for the inevitable with hands and whiskers aquivering violently.

The Augustinemonkmice moneylenders asked where she was.

'Who?' he replied innocently fully intending to walk briskly on.

'You know who, Angelica.'

Spike stopped and explained, both slowly and deliberately, that she was off work but this led to the biggest of the pair lifting him up effortlessly by the collar.

TC, watching this drama with his mouth hanging open, jumped forward but frantic arm signals from Spike, plus a strangulated garble, indicated that Ole should be fetched at once.

'Where is she?' demanded the pair.

Spike whispered that she was sick and asked them to come back next week.

'We will seize mousesonal possessions in lieu of so take us to her room!'

Spike asked to see their Bailiff's Permit, a sort of last ditch delaying tactic, but they replied with a painful combined head and arm lock that made him feel faint.

Then a cry rang out and the grip relaxed. Spike peered over his assailant's shoulder to confront, eyeball to eyeball, a very wild looking ladymouse in a rather well cut leather ensemble and wearing enough rattling jewellery to stock a used cart lot.

She was close, very close, and her arm reached through Spike's assailant's legs and gripped, something very mousesonal, tightly in her fist.

'Hello George,' she murmured quite pleasantly considering the circumstances. 'Still coming the bully boy then?'

His partner lunged forward and the ladymouse hissed; 'If my other hand goes into action I'll crack both his nuts and your dear friend will never sing bass in the monkmouse choir again.'

His partner moved back and Spike was tossed to one side. She kept a good grip on whatever to frogmarch the doubled up body, giving a good imitation of *Hunchcrutch Rides Again*, right up to the footbath and in.

One could not fault her arm movement, or follow through, as she rolled the fat bundle into the filthy water.

She stood over him, hands on hips, and said her piece; 'Listen to me you troglodyte and listen well. I'm taking over this debt and you will be told when the clock starts again. Now clear off.'

George grunted as he remembered past dealings with this wild one and knew that age had not mellowed her one iota!

'I take that as an affirmative,' she said and turned to find a crowd, which included Ole, TC and Old Harry, giving her a well deserved round of applause.

She inclined her head and that was Spike's introduction to Lisa the Anchoress.

Lisa and her group set about decorating the Cathedral for Xmas and TC, a talented reed flautist whose Mother had passed on the gift of a musical ear, said their singing was very good if only they stuck to traditional ditties and kept still.

With miniskirts that left little to the imagination, they sometimes caused the churchmice's thoughts to stray and Lisa had taken quite a shine to Spike. If she happened to be up a ladder, with him nearby, then a call would ring out through the air.

'Spikey!'

He would look up, in all innocence, and find himself greeted with an eyeful no respectable churchmouse should even think about!

An *m-mail due shortly* signal came through so Spike hurried along to the shop with MacDowell where, together with Brian, the three of them sat around the m-mail machine with their slates and chalks at the ready.

The machine was switched on and traces of Latin, Hungarian, French, and someone sounding very Welsh, came through as the various servers sprang into life. The staccatoed address boomed out; 'giovanni@salisburycathwilts.com' followed by a quiet period. The horn then started to spin, emitting a sort of swirly gurgle, and each mouse wrote down that part of the message that whizzed past his ear before the server finally signed off.

Spike collected up the slates and paid Brian before walking back to the office. Ole was waiting, already complaining that he was too old to learn this new technology but obligingly wrote down the text as Spike translated the slates.

From home was news of Aunt Maisie having had another of her turns and the castle siege seemed quiet with the two sides involved in negotiations. An answer to the m-mail regarding the hash crop was attached and then the news they had all been waiting for.

Uncle Zeb's secret instructions were written in a read once only script, which started to fade as Spike scanned the text and took notes.

The list of ingredients was discussed and they both agreed that the gathering of the odds and ends would require a collective effort involving everyone with a few favours being called in.

Old field and harvest mice, from the alms cottages and various shelters, were quizzed about the location of rarer plants and herbs while an old dormouse, who Victor had known as a ladmouse and considered a right wally, was paid a visit.

Snag, a specialist in *Aromapathic Corndollies*, might have helped with the alternative ingredients but was unable to stay awake long enough to hear the question so they left him slumbering.

The source for opium in Glasgow, according to MacDowell, was the Chinese Laundry so they assumed it to be the same in Salisbury. They spoke to a Mr Wu, who owned the local one in Salt Lane, but he was awaiting a shipment and didn't know exactly when it would arrive. The pair thanked him but, before they reached the door, Mr Wu had extracted a deposit from Spike's pocket for a Kung-Fu course starting shortly.

No Augustine would ever kick sand in his face again but he really wanted more time to think about it!

Lisa finally solved the opium problem by calling in a favour from the chief trader of the *Alchemy Soke*. It came in the form of pellets used in pipe smoking, which first had to be dried and crushed and Spike, sitting in the mixing room with his nerves all on edge, was visibly relieved when the final ingredient arrived.

His seemingly innocent remark of, 'I didn't know you smoked a pipe,' triggered off a chain of events commencing with Lisa showing him exactly how well she did smoke a pipe and ending with his mind definitely made up to take Mr Wu's Kung-Fu course!

He felt as if a tree had fallen on him and when Gerard arrived Spike's nerves were in a worse state and he told him, quite bluntly, to clear off as the formula was for the Italian Clothe only. Eventually he finished the mixing procedure and emerged from the office to find Ole waiting to escort the flask of precious potion. They arrived safely at the canteen and on to the patient's bedside where Margaret and the rest of the mice were anxiously assembled.

The stitches had worked around Angelica's ear and the whiskers, although healing slightly lop-sided, looked quite becoming. The swelling on the eye had reduced and the Mousedentist had looked at her teeth promising to cap the broken front one. However the periods of extreme agitation were severe with the carers unable to offer relief as nothing seemed to calm her down.

Margaret read the instructions on the flask;

'Commence with 2 drops each hour on a spoonful of honey until the agitations stop and wait for a while. Continue with 4 drops per spoonful for 2 hours and then the shock awakening which should cure the Sarlice.'

Lisa had known Angelica for a number of years, their parents having worked the markets together, and was very shocked by her friend's condition. She was reassured however that Uncle Zeb's potion should work and, after listening to the various ideas on how the *Shock Awakening* should be applied, suggested dropping the patient from a great height!

Ole told her to be serious and then, when the handymice discovered a huge ear trumpet in one of the cupboards, it was found to fit snugly over Angelica's head. Lisa said she would warble a few melodic bars of something rousing down the earpiece where, hopefully, the noise and vibrations should snap the patient out of whatever ailed her.

An occasional single nostril snort was the only sound as the patient lay in a deep slumber with the first part of the treatment completed as per instructions. The group reassembled to help Angelica up into the sitting position before placing the ear trumpet over her head. Lisa settled herself by the earpiece to await the signal, her lips all of a quiver, and the assembly fell silent in anticipation.

Ole raised his finger, nodded his head then Lisa, taking a deep breath and looking around, shouted down the earpiece at the top of her voice;

'Wake up you fat tart.'

No one saw the fist before it connected with Lisa's eye.

It came out of the swaddling bandage, picked up some serious momentum through an underhand swing and connected, boy did it connect!

Lisa staggered back and uttered a choking noise before collapsing on the floor, in a heap, with the ear trumpet lodged in her throat.

The patient stretched, sat up, rubbed her eyes then cracked her knuckles and asked;

'I'm hungry, what time is it?'

She noticed the assembly. 'Why are you all staring and what am I doing here?'

Ole stepped forward. 'Welcome back to the real world.'

He ushered the rest of the onlookers, apart from Margaret, out of the room enabling Angelica to come to terms with the immediate situation. Gerard helped MacDowell, who had managed to extract the ear trumpet, carry Lisa outside to a quiet spot in the Close where she could sit and recover from her bleeding eye and swollen lips.

Angelica listened quietly as Ole tried to explain that she had hurt her head in a fall but she, handling the dressings on her face, interrupted;

'Lordy, lordy me, I can't go out like this!'

She then noticed the look of disdain on Margaret's face.

'Never mind, I'll go back to my room thank you, I want to go now.'

Ole decided that she needed her own space with familiar things and so, silencing his wife's protest that the poor girl shouldn't be moved, went out to locate the wicker/wattle carry chair and two strong chapmice. This act of kindness resulted in Angelica soon being settled in the peace and quiet of her room.

The mice were assembled to discuss Angelica's condition and Ole suggested that all questions be referred back to him. He asked them to pray extra hard, even going into overtime prayer currently paying time and a third, that this awful episode would have an amnesiac quality with poor Angie remembering nothing.

Other important items were also discussed and he revealed that Potts had been spotted leaving the wine cellar late one evening. The delivery of laundry baskets to the safe house in the Close had increased so Lopes would be organising the wine sales from a safe distance.

However, Ole stressed the point; their greed would soon lead to the pair taking chances so he advised patience before action and an opportunity, to nail both Lopes and Potts, would arise.

He went on to say that the findings of The Ecclesiastical Court had ruled O'Rourke to be in serious breach of the Churchmouse Code of Conduct with desertion of his post, and bringing the service into disrepute, being the last straw. The alcoholic mouse had already been medically discharged and handed over to the Exouris Drying Out Clinic.

Ole concluded with the news that Brother Spikus' name had been put forward for an Exouris Pensionable Position. That statement caused Spike's back to be well patted and his health to be drunk on cracking open two bottles of '94' Chablis, full character with a rosey nosey and a dry clean finish, before the meeting broke up in time for tea.

Spike and Reggie were invited to eat at the top table. Ole usually dined alone but the wine had put him in the mood for company and there was business to discuss. Reggie explained, quoting Uncle Zeb's advice on the hash, that when the times of light and dark were reduced to six hours apiece, the plant would think it was day, then night, over a period of twelve hours.

The crop would fruit in half the time, twice per season and double the crop.

Top quality plants needed the full cycle so these would be a slightly inferior crop and it would be more labour intensive and expensive as more shade flax fencing would be needed. They agreed it was worth a try as the plague, although slowly moving north about, was still doing its rounds.

Angelica sat up in bed and tried to come to terms with the loss of five whole days out of her life. The dreams were so disturbing and, waking at all hours with the shakes and sweats, she felt awful. Regular close inspections of her face revealed that her servicing days could well be over as no one would pay for any favours and the debt hung over her like the hobs of hell.

She was interrupted however, in the midst of pouring a large tot from the flask, by a knock on the door and Lisa stood without, a bunch of droopy flowers in one hand and yet another flask of gin in the other.

'Lordy, lordy me, what are you doing in this neck of the woods. The sun is over the belltower and I was just going to pour a large gin, pray come and join me.'

Lisa did come in and sat on the bed where, as she moved by the candle light shade, Angelica could not help but notice that someone had messed up her face too.

'Lordy, lordy me, did you fall out of the tree as well?'

Lisa stood up and drew a breath. 'Don't you honestly remember?'

'Remember what?'

'Nothing,' was the reply.

'Look Lisa all I know is what Ole told me. If I fell then it must have been off the sodden church roof to get this sort of facial damage. It was pouring with rain, I lost a shoe in front of St Thomas' and that's all I can remember.'

The pair had had their differences in the past but, reaching out, Lisa hugged her friend.

'You poor, poor, dear,' she said and then asked. 'Haven't you anyone you can call on, how about that sister of yours?'

'Cheribina you mean. She's still serving at some pub in Eling and looking after the sailormice on the Test Barges so she's far too busy.'

Angelica gave a sniffle then suggested; 'Let's have that drink anyway,' and so, with the gin flowing freely, they talked and drank well into the night.

Spike was mentioned and they agreed he was a very fanciable commodity and the story of George, the Augustinemonkmouse, was told and re-told with them having a good chuckle but Angelica said he could make life difficult for her in the future but at the moment the debt pressure was off.

(Lisa did mention, as an aside, that his privates were very straggly, very droopy and painfully skinny despite his huge gut and she could only feel one!)

So what the hell.

They talked and talked about the many facets of life that ladymice find interesting and when they laughed it hurt but it did them good. The last flask was emptied as they decided to call it a day, or night, or early morning in fact before they staggered towards the gate. Lisa was pointed in the general direction of her sleepover and shared her parting wish to meet Spike who then just might carry her off to bed.

It crossed Angelica's mind, just momentarily, that she would scratch the tart's eyes out if she got to hear about it!

Epistle Five

Spike, Early December 1528

He awoke with a thumping great head and tried to remember what he'd been drinking at his belated birthday party the previous evening.

Someone found a bottle of home brew made from fermented swede peel, from which they all had sippers, and another someone suggested a kitty to buy a firkin of Mead so Spike went down to collect it. On the way back he slipped into The Belltower for a swift half and bumped into Jake and other sailormice who joined in his birthday celebrations and by the time he got back to the canteen, with a right skinful of *birthday brandies* under his belt, the rest were drinking *Old Harry's Gut-Rot* and anything else they could lay their hands on.

Other events came to mind as he buried his head in the pillow, but this did not help the feeling of dread from slowly spreading itself through his nether regions.

He wouldn't be so stupid–no——no——not that stupid. Surely not!

His concern stemmed from the main subject of discussion later that evening which happened to be the parachute and this had led to some pretty heated arguments, mainly with Gerard-Du, about the supreme relative knowledge of French and Italian inventors. This led him to jump on the table, in a burst of ridiculous arm waving patriotic passion, to proclaim his faith in Leonardo by offering to jump off the steeple wearing his wonderful invention.

No one would take that statement seriously, surely not on his birthday?

The solitude of the moment was ended with the voice of Gerard Du, outside the door, who asked how much Spike weighed.

'Clear off' was the answer but Gerard went on muttering, about wanting to work out the arc of descent and projectile velocity during the parachute jump, before silence fell once again.

The problem needed to be sorted now so he got up for a rinse, whisker brush, teeth clean and a *berry to clear all heads* washed down with water. He dressed and then, venturing gingerly outside, he peered around the corner to find Gerard had gone.

Wonderful, there was no one about, and then Reggie appeared.

'My friend,' a greeting followed by; 'I will give you something and you won't even have to climb the inside ladder. This weed is very special hand rubbed charas and one toke will float you through the spandrels and up to the steeplecross.'

Spike just growled and Reggie went, chucklingly, on his way.

Angelica sat in the canteen nursing the mother of all hangovers and, as her dreams had been most disturbing, she had taken over from Prudence until lunchtime. So, with two pots of tisane and wads of jam, Spike followed her to a table by the window to discuss the state of their respective heads and other important topics.

He tried to keep the conversation light with tales of last night's party and a few weak jokes about parachute jumps, and she did sense his compassion and discomfort but, when she realised he was averting his eyes from her face, still an awful mass of bruises and cuts, she broke down into body racking sobs. Ole happened to be passing the canteen window on his way to the office and, noticing her obvious distress, soon returned with Prudence. He took Angelica gently by the arm and walked her back to her room leaving Spike feeling like the absolute pits.

MacDowell then arrived to reveal that he had already opened a betting book for the jump and the money was rolling in. This confirmed Spike's worst fears and he swiftly exited the canteen desperately seeking a place with an ambience to rest his troubled mind.

Reggie joined him but sensed that Spike wanted to be alone so he handed over one of his specials and left. Spike wandered towards the meadows and lit up then wondered how Uncle Zeb would have handled the problem but he couldn't see the Chaplain's Corp having an Airbournemice Division!

Another drag replaced concern with clarity and, as his head hurt less when lying horizontal, he slumped down on the grass and looked up at the steeple. If the jump succeeded, he pondered, then his name would be written in posterity and a sponsored jump would definitely solve Angelica's money problems. Some financial good would then come out of it whichever way it went with beatification, at least, as an additional reward for failure.

St Spike or St Giovanni, much classier, and they would inter him next to St Osmond!

His thoughts wandered again as he tried to recall the difference, in the passing cloud patterns, between cumulonimbus and nimbostratus? Of course he knew but just couldn't remember and it was this mental effort that lulled him into a mid-morning nap.

He awoke after a while, sat up, and remembered having a bag of crumbs in his pocket for the birds. Various species flew in for this unexpected snack and, noticing for the first time that birds were ear-less, wondered how on earth they could hear. His thoughts turned to how easy flying looked, and then on to wondering if the fliegermaus could give him a few pointers.

He must make the effort to contact them.

Jumping on and off the bench, a sort of practice, failed to inspire as his heart really wasn't in it. Impending doom replaced euphoria as the effects of the hash started to wear off and so, rolling the crumb bag into a ball, he kicked it all the way back to the Cathedral.

Just because!

Anonymouse

A queue had formed in front of MacDowell's *book* where he sat scribing in the Diptych and wishing that O'Rourke, who could work out straight odds, reverse doubles, accumulators and combination wagers in his head, was still around.

Joe N, one of the handymice, held the bag and wrote up the odds on the wall as they were dictated. It was five to two that Spike would chicken out, seven to four that he'd kill himself, and thirty-three to one that he'd jump and live. The money kept rolling in as everyone wanted a wager ranging from a milli to mega groats. Lengthening the odds on Spike succeeding to a hundred to one, a town rat combined a *survival bet* with one of the sun shining on the day.

Fat George, of the Austins, put quite a heavy packet on Spike chickening out and he should have been told to take his money elsewhere but *the book* had to keep in their good books!

Better odds were requested on the method of Spike's demise. These ranged from being impaled on something very painfully pointy poking out the top of the North Transept and bleeding to death in front of hundreds of spectators to crashing through the tile roof of the Morning Chapel and breaking every bone in his body on the stone floor.

Side bets were placed on the specific incidents occurring;

(1) A heart attack or mental breakdown prior to the jump.

(2) Strangled by the parachute cords.

(3) Caught in a crosswind and never seen again.

(4) Fall on someone and have the pants sued off him.

(5) Trampled to death by the crowd.

(6) Ending up at least 25% shorter than what he was before.

Gerard, high in the steeple and completing a project feasibility study, had just finished doing his sums at the access door seven elles below the steeplecross. If Spike expected to jump out of this and, as the label said, *'float safely to earth without breaking arm, leg, or head'*, then he was in for one hell of a shock as he would definitely hit something on his way out and down.

He discussed it later with Ole and they both agreed that Spike and the roof would collide with unexpected speed and hardness so the projectile had to be projected cleanly out of the door at a very high velocity and the method selected was the *Mangonel*, a form of siege catapult.

This *boulder-slinging-over-the top-weapon*, in use and improved over the centuries, was a contraption that some of the older mice had seen but they knew nothing about its workings.

That was until Victor, searching through the family chest, came across some old drawings and sketches that his Grandfather had brought from Old Sarum. Leafing through he found one that showed several views of a working model of the Mangonel Siege Catapult.

A project work committee was hastily formed and they climbed up inside the steeple but then had to wait for the arrival of the elderly churchmouse as he took twice as long to manage the stairs. Mr Isaac, the Forehandymouse, had already sorted out lengths of timber left behind by the original builders, and these were inspected and selected pieces put to one side.

Victor was voted 'Project Manager', the original plans were his anyway and so, ably assisted by the team of building handymice, they then set about constructing a scaled version of the siege catapult christened 'Matilda' after the old mouse's Grandmother.

It was unfortunate to note however that another mouse, the only one on the committee vehemently opposed to Victor's selection, could bring the work to a grinding halt at such an early stage.

Victor was unable to abide French Mice in any shape or form and, although *The Higher Being* dictated that churchmice should love all other creatures, he found this rule extremely difficult to put into practice.

His animosity stemmed from the fact of not only disliking garlic, of which Gerard ponged quite strongly at times, but that his Auntie Josie had become pregnant by a French *'Monkmouse Diplomatique'*. The scoundrel had pleaded diplomatic immunity, took a posting to the Spanish Netherlands, and Auntie Josie never quite regained her *'joi-de vie'*!

The problems began when Gerard Du poked his size 13 into the building of Matilda; his accented drone ridiculing the given name, and continuing with statements like;

'In France we do it this way.'

Victor cracked one wet and windy afternoon and, with an agility surprising himself most of all, leapt at Gerard's throat to express his frustrations waving a razor sharp adze.

This led to both of them nearly pre-empting the jump, without the benefit of a parachute, as they fell against the top doorframe and very nearly out. The handymice managed to drag them inside to safety and Ole was sent for to sort out the situation.

Climbing all the way up to the steeple, coupled with the fact that he had far more important things to do, his heavy step heralded the arrival of the *Not-so-Happy-Mouse-in-Charge*. On reaching the top step, with his brow heavy with sweat, he sat and had a good grumble which put him in a better mood before inquiring into the causes of the dissension.

Both sides argued their case and Ole had difficulty in keeping neutral while Gerard Du rabbited on but he quickly came to a decision and gave the mice his verdict. Victor owned the plans so he was promoted to *BuildingMasterMouse* with the authority to hire or fire.

Gerard Du needed details of the mechanics of Matilda because, in conjunction with Spike's weight and the height of the door frame, the fulcrum point position, length of hurling arm, strength of the cord and the mass of the dropping stone all had to be calculated and the relevant drawing rolled off by MinuteMouse in the High Street.

Everyone agreed that Gerard was very good at that sort of thing but he should keep away from Victor and deal through the Forehandymouse.

Ole sat in at the weekly meeting with the Cathedral's hierarchy and was surprised, to say the least, when Mr Knyght congratulated him on his wonderful idea to swell the Cathedral funds by means of a parachute jump. This pleased the old mouse but then Mr Knyght asked him to explain, to the meeting, what a parachute actually was!

He tried his best to remember what Spike had read out and was thankful that no one questioned him on the principles of aerodynamics and other associated points about which he knew absolutely nothing. Before the meeting ended Ole requested that a Service of Thanksgiving, for the deliverance of Angelica's life, be held in the Chantry. Mr Knyght agreed but warned, owing to the plague, the *Sarisbarium* hymn of thanksgiving had to be sung *sub silencio* with all bells muted although voices and small musical instruments were allowed.

Musical ability amongst the Exouris left a lot to be desired with enthusiasm compensating for their obvious lack of skills. Ole had appointed himself as Micetro and was determined to put on a good show so he called a rehearsal with orders to bring either something to play or a voice to sing. TC was the only one who knew the meaning of *'Fugue'* so he was appointed leader. MacDowell brought his mouseorgan, Reggie his bongos and Lisa, with her group, comprised the vocals. Spike had not been gifted with the fine tenor voice of some fellow countrymice but still felt the need to contribute something to the music and felt most uncomfortable when Lisa kept throwing meaningful glances in his direction.

He was a professional churchmouse for God's sake, not your common and garden *'mouse ordinaire'*, and he was so relieved when Ole slotted him into the combined Critic and PR role which would keep his mind off Lisa and the parachute jump!

Gerard Du then arrived with a folding didgeridoo.

This surprised everyone and he pronounced the word very slowly several times as no one, including TC, had ever heard the name.

Spike got the closest with *'Digereedooda'*.

Gerard, the colour still not back into his cheeks after the steeple incident, told of buying the instrument from an itinerant ladymouse named Madge who wore corks around her hat. She had to sell her beloved didgeridoo to pay the Y.M.H. bill in Chartres and he became quite emotional saying he had sent postcards, plus a parcel, to her address at a place called *'Locae'*.

Witnessing the French mouse behaving almost normally made the rest feel embarrassed and uncertain of what to do next but Ole saved the day in bringing them all to order by tapping his baton and Gerard carried on assembling the strange instrument. He appeared to be wrestling with an octopus at times and the task took ages to complete but, after giving a few toots and a period of fine-tuning, a delightful deep resonant sound filled the Chantry.

The rehearsals started quite well, considering, and TC adjusted the tempo with his reed flute if any of the others fell behind. Reggie was missing quite a few of his bongs until Ole noticed that he seemed mesmerised by Lisa's legs. She was told to stop bobbing about or change into a longer skirt as her nether garments, the droopy bit in the middle anyway, was clearly visible for all to see!

Lisa agreed to keep still, and to let her skirt down a smidgen, if the Micetro would replace the phrase *droopy* with *a primrose path meandering along interesting places!*

Gerard had difficulty in changing scales as mice with big noses usually have small mouths and he couldn't move his mouth fast enough around the mouthpiece of the didgeridoo. The rest of the Mousicians, plus the cat, worked at the tempo to accommodate him but the *Fugue* went all to pot. When the Micetro finally regained control he indicated pointedly, with his baton, that Gerard should forget the medley and concentrate on the rhythm which sorted the problem.

Ole then remarked that the caption, *Music enables Mouse to live in Harmony with his Maker*, didn't seem to apply in this case!

During a break TC said that a violin or cello was needed to bond the group and Ole revealed that Johanne, a fliegermaus flight commander, played a mean violin and went on to explain, to the recent arrivals, that a fliegermaus flight had encountered appalling weather some time back during a trip from Spain to Transylvania and were blown miles off course.

A section was collectively struck by lightning and went down over the Channel but the rest just managed to reach the Cathedral with hardly a flieger left between them. Their dire distress enabled them to claim 'Port of Refuge' status and the Exouris cared for and fed them until they were well enough to continue their journey.

After that the flights would often call in to sleepover, bringing exotic gifts and delicious sweetmeats for the Exouris, and some would even hibernate in quiet corners of the steeple.

Victor had to note their locations, in accordance with the Cathedral Fireplan, and knew most of them and even spoke the language, so Ole promised to find out if Johanne's flight was in residence and, if possible, try to arrange another rehearsal.

Anonymouse

The area of clear shelving, illuminated by the lamplight, stood out starkly from the dust-laden surrounds of stacked bottles. It indicated that what stood there before didn't anymore.

'Some creep's filched my wine!'

The statement, most unecclesiastical, came from the Cellarer as he withdrew the tallow lamp from the space previously occupied by the bottles of his choice. His intended selection had been wine from Crappay, a little known English-speaking Canton in the Swiss Wetlands, and was to have graced the table of the Great Hall.

'Crappay d'or', racked from a reserve semi-demi tread, was impish by nature with a full palate lift and an aftertaste of plums and blackberries which is so unusual in a white. These qualities made it a most succulent partner for the roast swan, with its medley of songbird stuffing, destined to head the menu at that evening's banquet. The wine dissolved the ever so slightly salty pieces of succulent swanflesh into morsels of manna from heaven.

'This will just have to do instead,' muttered the Cellarer and selected the '22 Traminainer' from the Strasburg Region. He loaded the alternatives on to the rope lift where the scullions above awaited the order to raise and carry to the kitchen coolroom.

Le Clef, that famed French locksmith and temporary resident of one of the better areas of Salisbury, stood in front of the wine cellar door and scratched his head through a hole in his beret. Earlier that day the Office of the Cellarer had summoned him to the Palace to inspect a malfunctioning lock and insisted that a new one be fitted.

The Cellarer turned a deaf ear to his reasoning that the present one only required a good clean, as the locksmith could find no malfunction, and then a cursory inspection revealed that the door had been brought from Old Sarum so it was unlikely that a replacement lock unit could be found. The lockboy however, cleaning his master's tools in the immediate area, noticed that the lock on the adjacent laundry door was of a similar pattern and pointed out this fact.

His reward was a clip alongside the ear but, after measuring and comparing, the locksmith decided that the easiest option would be an exchange. The Cellarer acceded to this request and Tolitha the Laundry Maid was summoned to surrender her workplace key, plus the spare one from the Palace kitchen board, and a check in the odd key box revealed there were no others.

Le Clef soon finished changing the locks, and checked that both worked well, then returned the keys to the Office before brushing off his beret and heading home for a late lunch and a well-deserved glass of vin ordinaire.

Potts sat on his cart waiting for Tolitha to open up the laundry chute door. He usually delivered the clean linen later in the afternoon to find the door open and the laundry maid elsewhere. But today, by rearranging his schedule, her arrival was eagerly awaited with an anticipation visually obvious in his codpiece and a twinkle in his eye.

He really wanted to know her better!

A pair of queer vicars passing by arm in arm smiled sweetly and paused, in mid-stride, to drool over the quivering codpiece. He ignored them to ponder other matters and how the demand for illicit wine had increased rapidly. Lopes handed over a cut of the profits every few days, albeit begrudgingly, enabling the laundryman to add to his nest egg of ill-gotten gains stashed safely away in a hidey-hole down by the river.

Past experience had taught Potts that these wine shortfalls must be noticed and if he were fingered by Lopes trying to save his own skin, or anyone else, then an appointment with the Ecclesiastical Hangman might well be on the cards. A pre-planned move, to avoid such a date, would be most beneficial for his health.

The Cathedral clock struck two o'clock, he had waited long enough and swung his cart around to go but first noticed the sawdust on the floor and then that the adjacent cellar doors had similar lock plates. Lopes had given him the wine cellar key for use later that day when it was quieter, together with a list of requirements, and Potts wondered if it fitted the laundry door as well. He tried and it worked so the baskets were quickly manhandled inside, his codpiece adjusted to the work mode position, and he then hurried away for the next delivery.

Tolitha walked briskly back from the Cellarer's Office deep in thought as her lunchtime had been spent sorting out dirty keys and failing to understand the need to change the locks in the first place. She heard the squeak before the laundry cart came into view and so, slowing her pace, avoided the meeting with Potts. The linen for the evening's banquet had already been sorted and pressed so he must have got tired of waiting.

Just the thought of Potts gave her the heebie-jeebies and she now ensured that the chute door was opened before he arrived and closed again after he had gone. During her first few days in the job she innocently opened the chute with him standing nearby. He quickly pushed her down amongst the soiled linen but keeping her head, maiden or otherwise, she remembered the advice of her Mother and got the knee up first before following through.

The resulting effect amazed her as did the tears that sprang to Potts' eyes!

On reaching the Bishop's Palace she walked up the side path to the laundry and it had crossed her mind that the new key might not fit but, after a couple of turns this way and that, the lock slid smoothly into the open position and the first door was latched back. As she turned to latch the other she banged her leg on the linen baskets sitting on the chute.

She stared at them and wondered how on earth Potts got into the laundry.

This question was considered during her break as she selected a sandwich from her lunchbox, chopped up an apple into thin slices, and considered the situation between bites.

'The Frenchman, that's it, he must have left the door unlocked.'

The obvious was stated to the laundry walls that Le Clef had forgotten to lock up when he had finished. But the door had been locked on arrival, or had it?

She could have been mistaken though, what with all the fiddling about, so she must remember to ask the Frenchman the next time they meet.

Potts slid the key into the wine cellar lock later that day and twisted, first one way and then the other. It was taken out, put back and the same process gone through again.

Handles were rattled, re-rattled and then combined with aswearing, acursing and akicking of the door. The whole double frame shook but the lock would not budge.

Tolitha, working late below ground level in the adjacent laundry cellar trying to catch up with her daily quota, looked up towards the source of the noise as she folded a tablecloth onto the ironing board.

'Maybe the wind has got up,' she said to herself then wearily climbed the stairs to check that the doors were properly secured. The doorframe then shook violently, more foul language, and something tried to displace her key that was on the half turn but it held fast in the lock.

The Cellarer wouldn't use such dreadful language so who on earth was it?

A few more kicks and curses then it all went quiet.

Except for the squeaking of a cartwheel.

'Damn Potts!'

She was petrified for the moment but kept her nerve and peered through the keyhole to prove that her guess was right. The laundry cart disappeared into the gloom and it took Tolitha some time, plus another four candles, to illuminate her work area before she felt safe.

Cook, or one of her friends, would soon fetch her for kitchen duties so she removed the irons from the fire and sat down to pour some tisane into a glass.

It rapidly emptied itself owing to the shaking of her hand.

'What on earth did Potts think he was doing?'

She pondered over his strange behaviour and considered reporting him to the housekeeper but it was against her nature to cause trouble. After all he had only rattled the doors and poked something in the keyhole.

She managed a giggle to herself when she hoped it wasn't that!

An inside bolt would have to be fitted and, if she stood close enough to Monsier Le Clef whilst asking the small favour, he was sure to oblige

He had an eye for the ladies and the trick was not to stand too close.

A loud knocking followed by a familiar voice ended this line of thought and she opened the door to the smiling face of her friend Ada. The candles were snuffed, the door securely locked, and the two girls walked arm in arm back to the Palace Kitchens.

Later that evening Potts, sitting in the corner of his room, compared the key with the original lead casts and found no twists, bends or other abnormalities. His trying to pinpoint the problem then led to a disturbed night in bed and a gnawing feeling, in his bones, that this particular golden goose might not see the year out.

And the same feeling was soon to be shared with Lopes when he arrived, early the next morning, at one of the larger houses in the Close. He was to collect the payment for a wine order which, unknown to him, had failed to materialise the previous day for a very important evening meeting and the Curate, ignorant of the supply line hitch, walked blissfully right into *it*.

The House Butler, needing wine at short notice from a market experiencing acute supply problems, had been at his wits end when the order failed to show. Enter Claude, a manager from the Upper Snoutings, and a raving fruitcake to boot. With the obligatory drooling mouth and lascivious eyes, he let it be known that 'he had a little bit put by'.

Forced to oblige the manager in the role of the *'Gay Grovelier'*, the butler was then allowed to purchase the dregs of a definitely dodgy barrel of Chianti from the Sixpenny Handley Vineyards at a highly inflated price.

It is sad to note that the only agreement reached at that very important meeting, in one of the larger houses of the Close, was a unanimous decision soundly condemning the choice of the wine!

The next morning dawned and the House Canon was still furious with the butler whose nerves were already stretched to the limit. So when Lopes chose to ring the pantry doorbell he was quite unaware of anything being amiss.

One moment he was standing on the doorstep, hand outstretched, awaiting the feel of a brown parchment envelope. The next he found himself lifted off his feet, dragged inside by his dog collar, and bailed up against the hat-stand by an irate butler.

'What happened to the bloody wine?'

The question, spat through gritted teeth, came from a man who expected the Clothe to honour its word with the morals of the failed transaction a mere side issue. Lopes pulled away and tried to put his dog collar, and his neck, back to their original positions.

And the reply came from one who truly believed that the Clothe had honoured its promise;

'Of course the wine was delivered, you have my word on that!'

It was at this point that the Butler lost it and actually hung the Curate up on the hat-stand before storming out and slamming the door.

'Keys just don't stop working you pillock; give them here for me to try.'

Lopes had finally found Potts and, after listening to his tale of woe, spat out the reply.

Compensation to the butler had amounted to twenty groats, with a further five to the cook to fetch her brother to lift him down from the hat-stand, and any further breakdowns in the supply line did not warrant thinking about as his order book was bursting at the seams. The problem had to be sorted now and the errant curate gingerly approached his quest with a certain amount of trepidation as he could not be seen trying out illicit keys in strange locks in broad daylight.

Usually it was quiet at this time but there was a constant stream of major and minor officials into the Palace. Darkness and rain fell together and Lopes, feeling cold, wet and hungry, was thoroughly fed up as he only had to check that the keys worked and then Potts could carry on filling the order book. These thoughts were uppermost in his mind and, throwing caution to the wind, he walked towards the Palace and hurried up the side path.

At the cellar door he paused and looked around. No one about so, using his cloak to conceal, he slid the key into the lock and turned. He tried anyway, first one way and then the other. An approaching cleric, closing fast, spurred him into a final twist that resulted in a sharp metallic crack.

He stared for a moment at the broken keyshaft in the lock before tossing the useless end away and walking slowly back down the path.

Gerard's Didgeridoo

How a Didgeridoo happened to find its way to Chartres was an unfathomable mystery and it wasn't solved until I met Gwindowlina, a fellow early morning swimmer at the Five Rivers Leisure Centre, who eventually enlightened me on the subject.

She was employed as a shelf-filler but insisted that she was in line for the next vacant cashier's position at that well-known supermarket that no one has a good word for but everyone seems to patronise.

I mentioned my story, as narrators often do when they have a captive audience, whilst we were both in the outer changing room and she replied that she had sat her GCEs with Geography and History amongst the subjects passed.

It soon became obvious to Gwindalina, who only wished to dry her feet and go, that she needed to address my queries about the Didgeridoo if she had any chance of getting to work on time so she reckoned that it arrived as follows;

The Portuguese Explorer, Ferdinand Magellan, was selected to lead a flotilla of 5 cruise ships around the world. The expedition, funded by the King of Spain, was supposed to be an opportunity for his friends to invest in a gilt edged venture but unfortunately Ferdy got himself involved in a pub brawl in Cebu and drew his last breath before it was sorted.

His trusty Mate, Sebastian del Camo, carried on bravely to complete the circumnavigation but only managed to arrive back with one ship, the Victoria. He spent the rest of his life trying to explain what had happened to the rest!

Somewhere along the way however a large chunk of land, what is now thought to have been the North Western Coast of Australia, was sighted and christened *Locae*.

There is no official record of them actually landing as the King of Spain struck the record of the sighting from the vessel's logbook although he was supposed to have remarked;

'It sounds an awful place, leave it for English Henry to discover!'

Anyway they could have anchored in one of the bays and taken the longboat ashore for a few cans of Fosters, a bit of a singsong, and a quick leg-over. They then brought back on board, in addition to numerous doses of clap and other seafaring maladies, a local trophy in the shape of Madge, her hat of hanging corks, and her beloved *Folding Didgeridoo* safely tucked away in its rucsac.

Epistle Six

The Curate's Comeuppance

He considered his options whilst watching his cassock, cloak and boots drying by the fire in the back parlour of St Thomas'. They did not look healthy but Lopes held a grossly overrated belief in his own infallibility and earning a crust elsewhere would be no problem as he would be ministering to the majority existing on the very edge of the law.

And he had the advantage of being completely scruple free!

Gifts, a few groats maybe, would always be available to be pledged, via his good self, to the Church by a people desperate for any member of the Clergy, bent or otherwise, to comfort the dying, hear confessions, or be in attendance at the expiration of life to give the last rites. The prudent shyster would have grabbed a bag and jumped the first cart or ass but Lopes had one last card to play that would fatten his purse at the expense of the lowly paid domestic staff of the Close.

He then dressed for bed, in his *'God loves me above All'* nightshirt with matching cap and bedsocks, and immediately fell into the dreamless sleep of the untroubled and the innocent.

'Mon Dieu, this is all I need.'

This sigh of frustration was directed at Gerard Du who'd noticed something going on at the Wine Cellar and had joined the small crowd of onlookers along with MacDowell.

'Why don't you try pushing it through?' the French mouse suggested.

Le Clef, who felt no affinity towards his fellow country creature whatsoever, had been inserting an assortment of picks and tools into the lock, without success, since the early hours and had even chastised the lockboy for not having fingers thin enough to grasp the end of the broken key.

The locksmith was at the end of his tether but he patiently explained that this type of key had a location stop so it couldn't be pushed through.

Gerard knew this to be untrue, being familiar with every crook and nanny of this particular key, but bided his time as the locksmith continued to fiddle.

'Why don't you just try it?'

A pointed file was then waved, quite aggressively, in Gerard's face.

'Because-it-won't-work.'

These staccatoed words were spat out as the locksmith took a lunge at the lock and MacDowell, telling the story later in the canteen, said he was reminded of a rapier-waving beret-wearing lunatic.

Metal dropping on stone, the sound emerging from the other side of the door, must have been heard in every corner of the Close.

'Feel free to call on us at any time Mon Ami.'

The statement, by MacDowell unable to keep a straight face, seemed to hang for ages in the air as the pair strolled away to continue their early morning walk.

The lockboy had been sent back to the workshop, under the threat of instant dismissal if one word was mentioned of this slur on his Master's professional pride, and Le Clef lent against the wall to examine the broken key and wonder who could have created such an abomination.

He then felt a hand on his shoulder and turned to find Tolitha, standing pleasantly close by, who asked that a slide bolt be fitted to the inside of the laundry door.

And she went on to mention that he had left the door unlocked yesterday morning.

The episode with Gerard Du had already left his ego somewhat shattered but this was too much. She continued to chide him about getting forgetful in his old age, but he categorically confirmed that both the doors were locked and both had been double-checked before double-checking them again.

She hadn't meant to upset him so she snuggled up and threaded her arm through his. He could feel her firm breast together with the nipple, erect like the G flat stop on the Cathedral organ, pushing into his arm. Her hot breath...

NARRATOR'S NOTE; Now where was I!

Tolitha recounted the tale of finding the baskets on the chute and Potts' later odd behaviour of poking something into the lock. She added that she couldn't be certain if the broken key was in the cellar door lock next to the laundry when she left that evening and took her own key from her apron pocket. Le Clef compared it with the broken one, it was similar so he surmised that it had been another attempt on Potts' part to make her acquaintance. But why try it in the wine cellar door where he only succeeded in breaking it off. They returned to their respective duties with that nagging feeling that something, like a misshapen key, didn't quite fit.

Lopes was up at first light to make his way to the Coaching Inn where he purchased a seat on the midday coach to Exeter, with funds rifled from the 'St Thomas' Xmas Appeal for the Needy' collection box, and stowed his carrybag in the loading bay.

He returned to St Thomas' and, after a hearty breakfast, entered the Chapel to ask God's forgiveness at the altar. He added that if God could save his butt this one last time then he would serve the Church, unbendingly, until the end of his days.

Norman stood quietly in the shadows watching a performance that he'd witnessed many times before but, on this occasion as he related later to Ole and MacDowell, God replied;

'Not a chance sunshine!'

Lopes heard it too and purposely farted. He wiped his mouth, spat on the floor, and walked out of the front door for the last time. In his haste however he missed a headshake from a disciple in the 'Doom' painting above the altar.

St Jude, the patron saint of hopeless cases, had tried to tell him something.

A signal from the tower, 'Subject heading in your direction,' was observed by Scrimshaw on duty at the Main Gate. A handymouse runner alerted Ole and Spike who were discussing the broken key over a working breakfast, and they puzzled over the motives of a man whose future wellbeing was definitely at risk around the Cathedral end of town.

Lopes, cloak a-flying and exuding confidence, strode from the High Street into the Close to take deposits for orders that he had no hope of fulfilling. The houses that had already paid were avoided but the others were fair game and one query, about the broken key, was met with such indignation that the man ended up apologising. It is a sad reflection on the gullibility and greed of the clergy to report that the scam was successful and the Curate, with a pocketful of groats and a spring in his step, walked out of the Cathedral for the last time.

Meanwhile on the other side of the Close in the Laundry basement a tub stands empty where, an hour or so before, Algernon Potts stood tubbing. News of the broken key was quickly common gossip so he waited until his early break to hang up his smock and briskly depart towards his lodgings where his landlady's suspicions were allayed as he told of a father, on his deathbed, calling for his favourite son. All his worldlies were quickly packed into a shoulder sack, his precious groat-stash recovered from its depositary, and then the laundryman strode off at a fair rate of knots south along the riverbank and in the general direction of Christchurch.

Lopes' every move around the Close had been monitored by Ole and Spike from the Control Centre assisted by the handyscouts on standby since dawn. The 'A' team, slipping smoothly into their '*seek to find*' mode, had reported at regular intervals with each piece of information assessed and it was soon concluded that the rest of his customers were being ripped off.

This was to be Lopes' day of reckoning.

An envelope, containing a small note scribed in an even smaller hand, was pushed through the letterbox of the safe house. It was deciphered using bottle top spectacles and revealed that Lopes had collected more deposits and then asked if the reader had had his share. The Canon, suffering from a bad dose of flu, visibly blanched blanchier than the normal flu blanch on realizing that others knew of his involvement with Lopes.

Who could write so small?

He thought of all the small people he knew, the little people, any larger people with small hands or it might even have been one of the Exouris. He'd actually been at that very important meeting, where the abominable cooking wine had been served, and it was obvious that there were serious supply problems with Lopes' scheme so his later attempts at sleeping had been one long nightmarish dream of hanging from the steeplecross by his goolies.

The Canon's blood pressure started to rise as he mentally, and spiritually, castigated himself for his past behaviour. A chance encounter at The Holy Trinity Weird Practices Club in Wilton had left him unable to refuse Lopes' request for storage facilities.

This train of thought went on to consider the possibility of Lopes being apprehended by the Authorities as he had recently read, in the 'S&M Monthly', of the latest addition in that very line.

'A *funnybone cracking and imploding spike*' had been voted the star selection, an item that no decent inquisition should be without, so an Ecclesiastical Model might well be used to help the errant curate straighten his story.

That train of thought was interrupted by the resonant bass voice of his housekeeper as it shimmied towards him in a new patterned kaftan, with matching shawl, and complemented by a dark eye make-up and a smidgen of colour on the cheeks.

'Like a cuppa or something darling?'

'No thank you Blanche, I am just on my way out.'

A theatrical flourish followed as it moved to his side and he gave that delightfully tight little bottom a playful squeeze before making his way slowly along to the hat-stand.

He pulled up his hood against the driving rain and, skirting the edge of the Green, headed towards the Main Gate. Lots of people were going the same way and the Canon wondered if he'd somehow got mixed up with the Xmas Parade. Some of the crowd he recognised, minor canons and vicars, but the majority were domestics and housekeepers alerted when the broken key story became public knowledge.

Any financial loss to the house funds would be their responsibility, and the loss made good from their own wages, so they were quite understandably *'Piqued off'*!

At St Thomas' the crowd circled left, following the boundary fence, then joined up again at the front gate. A seething group of angry humanity ringed the Church as they eagerly awaited their prey to appear while the Canon, desperately wanting to leave, felt compelled to stay and witness the outcome.

Judging by the mood of the crowd, plus the size of the meat skewers they were waving about, his trial and punishment would not be quick, or painless with disembowelment on the menu just for starters. Then news came through that Lopes had been sighted boarding the Noon Coach and the crowd, determined to see justice done just this once, moved en masse towards the Coaching Inn.

The Exeter bound coach sat parked outside the City Gates and the driver had just swung himself up onto the top seat after paying the clearance dues.

'All set then?' he cried as he released the hand brake and spread the reins.

The coach had yet to pick up momentum when the driver heard a commotion breaking out behind him. He turned towards the source of the noise and a head appeared at the window below to bellow;

'Drive man drive, this is no concern of ours.'

Lopes' words filled the air as the driver, concentrating once again on the job in hand, urged the team up to a fast gallop. With the rein leather cracking and sparks beginning to fly out of the rear near-side wheel hub, the coach cleared the City Environs.

The Keeper of the Key had never seen a crowd so angry at arriving late for the coach's departure. He erred on the side of caution, telling his guards to keep them out for the moment, but the crowd had noticed the sparks while Lopes chose to ignore them for obvious reasons.

Until the wheel hub overheated and seized.

In quick succession it detached itself from the axle and the coach slewed to one side but remained upright. The curate, who never bothered to fasten his safety belt, was propelled through the window to land on his head while the rest of the passengers remained safely strapped in but unhurt. When the dust had settled after such a grand finale they all climbed out of the coach, picked up Lopes, and trudged along the path from whence they came.

The crowd hushed as the passengers, followed by a few hands carrying the luggage, approached the Keeper where the driver asked permission to re-enter the City and a refund of his fees. This was done and the passengers, with their luggage, passed through the Gates and headed for the Coaching Inn to await the next service.

All except the Curate who, unable to comprehend the here and now, was handed over to his friends and firmly escorted back to the Cathedral.

And the Canon?

He walked slowly back to the house and the welcoming arms of Blanche who, if he played his cards right, might just be on for an afternoon session and a big cuddle.

NARRATOR'S NOTE; For sake of good taste I have deleted mind-boggling details of what the Clergy actually get up to in these Wilton clubs.

Anonymouse, Xmas thru New Year 1529

The festive season arrived before the staff realised and was over just as fast. The hours were long and the canteen, where the mice could find a warm fire, always had hot food and drink. Angelica seemed back to her old self and even more so when the Mousedentist turned up to cap her front tooth. Working with Prudence, shift about, they even found spare blankets to cover the mice when they dropped off exhausted over their pots of tisane and hot soup.

Ole and Margaret organised a Carol Service and the team assembled on Xmas Eve, before the Mass, to share a cup of good cheer. The rain was bucketing down and it was blowing a gale but they lit their candles, sang the seasonal hymns with great gusto, and remembered absent friends. Gerard Du handed out his Christmas Design Size 13s with Spike asking for a second one and then another; those Italianates were very emotional!

Mr Knyght failed to turn up for one of the services owing to mix up of the timetable and the relief organist, or the Cantor, couldn't be found either so the Precentor asked TC to lead the Vicars Choral with his reed flute.

It was a proud moment for all the mice when one of the Exouris came to the rescue on such an auspicious occasion culminating in a standing ovation and a vote of thanks. TC had definitely become a most useful member of the staff despite the orange streak and nose ring!

A strut tendon in Johanne Maus' nearside wing had sustained a hairline fracture after a miscalculation of the thermal downdraft necessitated a forced landing amongst the rocks. The flight had been surveying ley-lines but the rest managed to piggyback him to a staging post in time to pull the last cracker at the Xmas Day Supper. This setback meant a postponement of the Service of Thanksgiving as replacement items from the Central Fliegermaus Store in Transylvania, for the older staff members anyway, always took much longer to locate and supply because the parts were stored in a box located right at the back of the shelves.

Victor sent a 'get-well soon' card which was much appreciated.

The Xmas decorations were taken down and neatly folded into bundles before storing away in a dry cupboard. Lisa and her group were still helping on a casual basis and Spike was detailed to collect the pieces from the highest points using the tallest ladders.

'Why me?' he always asked when he already knew the reply. 'All good practice!'

It was over three weeks since Lopes had been officially sighted and certain mice on the staff, gifted in the art of scaremongering, took great pleasure in terrifying their companions of a more delicate nature.

They related tayles of screams and moans coming from the cellar of the Bell Tower and Reggie, whilst pushing his cart along the wall, experienced a skeletal hand making a grab for his foot. He then flatly refused to go near the place and even the natural bulging of his eyes seemed more prominent than before. And the CathCats, who usually slept through any catastrophic event, also reported their slumbers had been disturbed by the noise.

After thirty days Lopes' name was posted as 'Missing Presumed Lost' on the Lost and Found notice board and two of the minor clergy carried on caretaking at St Thomas' with the Incumbents due to return shortly.

The Cathedral hierarchy also decided to sort out the Graveyard Gang so, after them ignoring a 24-hour eviction notice and roughing up the handy-mouse who served it supposedly under a flag of truce, Ole was given the power to act as he saw fit. Volunteers were then called for, from amongst the Exouris and Laymice, to form a late night raiding party.

The rewards would be double time from commencement to completion and the next day off. Margaret forbade Ole to take part so Spindrift and Scrimshaw, along with Erskine and MacDowell, set off under cover of darkness with Reggie's cart to carry the body bags.

'B' troop of the Handyscouts, who had reconnoitred the graveyard area earlier in the day, acted as pathfinders. The operation was a complete success with the Scotsmouse returning twice during the night for more bodybags and it took quite a few

wash days to get the blood-stains out of the partici-
pants Ecclesiastical Camouflaged Fatigues!

Spike, Early February 1529

He woke in the early hours bathed in sweat after a
disturbed night of tossing and turning with his
whiskers all of a quiver. The wintry sun, struggling
to lift its weary head over a leaden horizon, shone
cheerless rays of early light through the windows of
'Cell Eight' and illuminated the picture of misery sitting on his bunk. There seemed to be no escape
from fate's harsh reality as he sat, wrapped in a blanket and waiting for, as the label caption read, '*The
Anti-Whisker Quivering St John's Wort Berrybalm*' to
take effect.

His feelings towards his Mother had triggered this
massive nosedive in his spiritual wellbeing and
down into the pothole of depression. He loved her
but the nagging doubt persisted that she was the
indirect cause and if she had only asked what he
wanted for his birthday, then a parachute would
have been the last choice. Uncle Zeb had described
the sketches of Da Vinci's ideas one evening at home
and Spike remembered wishing he could be the test
pilot on that project but that was only to impress the
girlmouse from next door!

A further concern was the indisputable fact that
he was terrified even though he joined in the lively
discussions and, after a few drinks, bathed in the
limelight.

It caused him hot flushes of fear that made putting
on a brave face difficult and played havoc with his

digestion. Reggie was in empathy but his specials, and an escalating dependence on the berrybalm from the Alchemist, had convinced Spike that his brain cells were dying as a few days ago it had taken him all morning to translate a simple Latin script.

The Alchemists were members of 'The Alchemy Soke', one of the so-called Honourable Guilds, and Spike felt, quite strongly in fact, that the members should behave in an honourable fashion. He objected to paying the prices demanded by those already dispensing worse than useless cures to a terrified population where families were willing to mortgage their souls, even their wives, daughters, and sons, in the hope of plague protection.

One in five people observing basic hygiene rules and in the immediate area of contamination seemed immune from the effects. The rest however, maybe observing the same rules of hygiene or better, succumbed when the plague was at its worst.

There was no hiding place from this terrible scourge once fate, selecting a town, village, or farm almost at random, paid it a decidedly unwelcome visit. City Walls, built primarily for protection from without, became a prison as authorities used draconian methods to stop the plague from spreading into uncontaminated parts of the country.

If one did manage to flee then it was to a place where the grim reaper reigned and the dead lay unburied and any approach to a 'clean' town was met by the threat of either a spear up the backside or an arrow through the eye socket.

The hint was usually taken.

Spike's thoughts returned to the present as he climbed off his bunk and made his way to the raredorter for his first port of call. The berrybalm stimulated his waterworks system resulting in a visit two or three times during the night and, if he had a few drinks in the evening, then he never seemed to be out of the place.

He had decided to lay his cards on the table so, as he passed MacDowell on his way to the lavatorium, he asked to have a word with him. If he was called *'That Gutless Eyetie'* then it was a small price to pay for his life and health but no way would he do the jump. He was willing to stand up in front of his peers, his head held high, and shout out loud that he was a cowardly, cowardly custard. Tradition deemed that a round of drinks be bought, the parachute then burned in Reggie's fire, and the whole sorry incident relegated to the realms of fantasy where it belonged.

'Yer Ferkin Wat?'

Spike stepped back sharply as MacDowell, his whiskers bent double and tail whipping in a vicious arc, reacted to his statement.

He repeated though not with quite the same forcefulness he managed the first time.

'Not doin the ferkin jump?'

The Glaswegian accent became more pronounced.

'Do ya know how much money is riding on this?'

Spike shook his head.

'Megagroats. The whole country's got a wager, some of them so big that I've had to lay them off with William Hillamouse.'

Spike's whiskers started to quiver violently and he desperately looked around for somewhere to sit before he fell. MacDowell felt compassion as he watched his friend stagger away but he alone knew the source of some of the wager groats.

And Spike's absence on the day would be a definite health hazard for both of them!

A few days later a staff meeting was held in the canteen. The subject under discussion was Spike's recent work record, in danger of having a permanent black mark added, and possible short listing for a punishment posting as his 'sickies' had increased tenfold since Xmas.

They knew where the trouble lay and the mice felt empathy for him but, as MacDowell pointed out, a great deal of hard work had been done and a huge amount of money laid out on the bets. Although this was earning a good rate of interest, in the Exouris Credit Union, they had to announce a date soon and only death or permanent disablement could cancel the event.

The Scotsmouse revealed that a percentage of the clear profit from the betting would be Spike's to keep anyway and confirmed that it would be paid posthumously, in the event of the worst scenario, to whoever benefited from his will.

The ChairMouse then opened the floor for questions where a plan was formulated to prepare our mouse, both spiritually and physically, for the task that lay ahead.

Spike sat on his bunk contemplating his feet sticking out from the bottom of the blanket. They needed a good wash but he had neither the desire nor the energy to get up or even move as all interest in daily life, religious or otherwise, had fast evaporated. Even the parachute jump had ceased to be of any concern and the earlier bouts of whisker quivering had stopped.

His worry mode gradually shut down as he convinced himself that one day they would come, carry him up to the steeple, and throw him out of the door. This, as far as he was concerned, couldn't come fast enough so he could be free of this awful life.

And it came to pass that this very poor facsimile dragged himself out of bed to splash water on his face, failing to brush whiskers, hair or teeth, before sticking grubby feet into even grubbier sandals. The soup and custard stains down the front of his cloak were glaringly obvious but he just couldn't be bothered to wipe them off.

It was in this appallingly scruffy state, a state where his illustrious ancestors would have cartwheeled in their graves that Spike, reacting solely to the pangs of hunger and not the breaking of bread, shuffled along to the canteen.

Angelica caught Ole's eye as our hero shuffled into view and, asking after his health, was rewarded by a rude grunt in reply. Tears came to her eyes and she felt the urge to gather him up in her arms, after giving him a good bath that is, and she nearly broke down as the covered lunch dish was handed over.

Cottage pie was the dish of the day, which happened to be one of Spike's favourites, so it was with anticipation that he sat down and lifted the cover.

The meal consisted of a slice of cucumber with a piece of tomato on a lettuce leaf.

And a prune on the side for dessert.

He looked up.

Everyone in the place seemed to be staring at him.

He bowed his head again and tears fell amongst the 'Healthy Option'.

Someone joined him at the table.

It was Ole whose bulk mercifully blotted out the rest of the mice.

Spike looked up into the face of his friend and spoke;

'Life's a bloody disaster, I need help.'

Epistle Seven

Operation Spikemend

He scrubbed himself from top to toe with Angelica's special scented soap and the hot water from the shower rose permeated new energy into every pore of his body. A pile of fluffy towels lay on the chair along with freshly laundered underwear and a clean cloak. Even his sandals had been cleaned, fumigated, and highly polished.

A counselling course had been hurriedly arranged, for the purpose of putting things of lesser importance right out of his mind, so Spike could concentrate on reaching peak condition over the next few weeks. He had neither the energy nor the wherewithal to resist and his workmates were told not to mention the parachute jump in any shape or form and just to offer assistance if he needed help keeping to 'The Plan'.

And this was just the first stage of 'Operation Spikemend'.

There was a spring in his stride as he walked briskly down to the Main Gate to meet Angelica and TC. Life had definitely changed, once that first step was taken, and a few days of strict diet and exercise made him feel so much better. And the first step, according to Ole, was the 'Healthy Option' that Spike had eaten in two mouthfuls.

She was waiting, looking very dishy in a tailored cloak with a rather daring side split and then, escorted by TC, they all walked down to the market place. It was the first Saturday in February and a lot of the shops were having a '*Say Hello to Spring*' sale but Angelica, who knew where the real bargains could be found, steered them towards the Cistercian Monkmice Opportunity Shop.

Rows of 'Pre-Loved' clothing and shoes overwhelmed them so she selected a few quality vests, a pair of 'Zife' jogging pants, an 'Ababas' loose jogging top and a pair of 'Luma' Trainers which fitted Spike perfectly. And there was even change from the two groat piece that Angelica took from his pocket to pay!

They had a good look around the market and then, leaving TC at the Cathedral Gate, carried the parcels back to the cell where Angelica insisted on a full dress rehearsal which was partially to make certain it all fitted and that he felt comfortable in these unfamiliar clothes. The other reason was that she rather fancied mice wearing running gear and regularly watched the sailormice jogging along the riverbank first thing in the morning.

She had drawn the short straw, from amongst the *Exouris*, to escort Spike over the weekend and to keep him in good spirits so, for today, why not?

Ole's orders were 'non-specific' but emphasized that Spike's health, both mental and otherwise, had to be sorted in the shortest possible time so, with the pillows fluffed up on his bunk and the candles snuffed, the stage was set for another important aspect of his treatment.

He was stretched out on his bunk and re-living the previous few hours.

Angelica's efforts, and what fantastic efforts they were, had dispelled the remaining gloom and placed him firmly on the right path. He sat up, intent on sorting out his jogging gear from the heap at the bottom of the bed, but as he folded the items on to a shelf he spontaneously decided to do the first run there and then.

MacDowell and Reggie, both looking very much the worse for wear, arrived back from the Bell Tower to find Spike stretching his quads and hams in the porch. He felt a bit of a wally in his new kit but the pair agreed that he looked very sporty indeed. They tried, really hard, to keep a straight face but when one started to laugh then the other was bound to follow.

He stood his ground for a while and then, without another word, turned on his heel and strode back to his cell and stood for a while blinking away the tears. However the family motto kept returning through the mist loud and clear; *'Above all, never stand on trifles'*, so he wiped his face and returned to the porch where the two mice sat somewhat shame-faced and feeling sorry for their behaviour. Ole's orders had been forgotten in an alcoholic haze so the runner walked by, his cloak over his jogging gear, and bade them both goodnight with a loud *'Stuff You'* before warming up to half speed and disappearing into the night.

Ole, Early February 1529

He sat in his office reading reports of the Pope's expected demise and that The Lord Chamberlain, Cardinal Wolsey, had left for the Vatican on a two-pronged mission.

The first was to persuade the Pope, before he died, that a dispensation to allow Henry to divorce Katherine and marry Anne Boleyn would be most beneficial for all concerned. The second prong was to point out that the ideal choice for the next Pope, according to Wolsey and a few of the hired help, was none other than Wolsey himself.

Ole shut the report and let out a weary sigh, signalling the end of his working day, before snuffing out the candles and locking the office door.

He first heard, and then spied, a figure running along the Close Wall and waited in the shadows for it to catch up. Out of the gloom emerged, before anything else took shape, some strange sort of footwear coloured blue and white. They seemed to have a mind of their own, glowing in the dark, and were about to pass when Ole recognised the wearer.

It was Spike and he called out a greeting.

The panting and puffing mouse came to a halt and slumped against the nearest wall with sweat pouring off his whiskers.

'Are you alright?' his boss enquired.

Spike nodded.

'For God's sake take your cloak off then, you must be roasting.'

Spike caught his breath and obliged revealing his rather snazzy outfit.

'What on earth are you wearing?'

'It's my outfit for getting fit.'

'Getting fit, getting fit, you look like the Court Jester. Where on earth did it come from?'

Spike explained the events of the afternoon and Ole calmed down enough to tell him to return the outfit before they all became the laughing stock of the town.

And, if it was exercise he wanted, then a brisk morning walk should do the trick!

A definite chill was in the air during the Sunday Services and the Monday started with Angelica banging down his breakfast on the table. The rest of the day was spent being ignored and Ole, knowing the reason, could do nothing to alleviate the problem.

He pondered the discussions to get Spike back on the right track but him appearing out of the blue, after a very tiring day, in that ridiculous jogging outfit just tipped his balance of sanity.

It was Spike who had to jump from the steeple so he should wear whatever he liked and Ole regretted that it was his one thoughtless remark that had cocked things up.

Later that evening however a group came running alongside the Close Wall just as Ole was, again, in the process of locking up. Led by Angelica, with Victor hobbling behind, all the mice were there with footwear glowing in the dark and Spike was the only absentee.

Dressed in various coloured tracksuits plus matching 'glow in the dark' trainers, he was greeted in unison as the group passed at a brisk trot and then they were gone.

He scratched his head and decided to visit the Snoutings on his way home. If you can't beat them then why not join them!

Next day seemed normal as a status quo had been reached and he admitted, but only to himself, of speaking out of turn in respect of Spike's running. A few turned out for the morning run and Angelica rewarded him with a big smile at breakfast time. The Court Jester remark was consigned to the past and Ole later heard that the Cistercian Shop had given a bulk discount, plus a further 10%, when Angelica explained it was for a *'Show of Solidarity'*.

She was reimbursed for any *'out of pocket'* expenses as the running gear could be utilised for work and worn under their cloaks on cold days. Margaret even bought a couple of track bottoms, to wear under their cloaks, which Ole said helped keep out the cold.

One problem did arise out of this but Angelica soon sorted it out. There were complaints from some of the Bell Tower customers of Reggie showing too much *'Builders Cleavage'* when leaning on the bar. An overall shape, which could only be described as *'Plum'*, meant that his jogging pants never managed to hang right around the waist.

Angelica rectified this by sewing in a large buttonhole at a lower level through which he could then, decently, thread his tail.

The rest of the week passed uneventfully until the Friday when, sitting in his office with three lighted candles as it had got so dark, his concentration was disturbed by a soft knock.

'Come in.'

No response so he walked to the door and opened it.

'Snuffen-zee oot der candle,' said a voice beyond the loom.

And continued; 'Ich bin Herr Johanne Maus von FliegerMaus Flug.'

The candles were snuffed and the caller invited into the office.

'Mind that chair, please sit down.'

Ole, unable to see a thing, then fumbled his way around the desk and sat.

Someone sat down opposite with a bump so he asked; 'Good flight back?'

'Ja, Ja, Danke, sehr gut.'

Ole asked to speak French as his Austro-Hungarian was not at all fluent.

'Mais oui,' was the reply and points about the Thanksgiving Service were first on the agenda. Johanne said he would be pleased to contribute his music but asked that the lamps be subdued as his senses went off balance in any light and he continually bumped into things. Amongst his Xmas presents however were a pair of shades, the latest wrap around style with self-darkening lenses, and maybe these would solve the problem.

He talked of the Siege and indicated that it would be all over in a month or so. The excommunication of Martin Luther, together with the Saxony Protesters, were discussed and they agreed on the subject of simony and the purchase of indulgences.

The subject of the parachute jump came up and Johanne said he might be able to help but would have to consult his companions first. Victor had shown him Matilda and he went on to say that The Creator, in his wisdom, set some creatures on earth to walk about and others to fly. Some were able to do both quite easily but Spike, unfortunately, happened to be a *wingless version*.

Ole suggested the next evening for a rehearsal but Johanne asked for a few days grace enabling his violin some time to become acclimatised. With that he stood and, clicking his heels together in a very smart fashion, bade Ole *'Gute Nacht'*.

As his visitor departed into the gloom Ole's thoughts drifted to simony and the purchase of indulgences. So called believers could get away with doing awful things to others and the Church aided and abetted on payment of a few groats to the Pardoner.

He shut the weekly accounts ledger and shivered, not from the cold though, but through the feeling in his bones that the winds of change were not too far away.

Spike, Late February thru March 1529

He was approaching the peak of his physical and mental fitness, plus feeling more *'with it'*. Familiarization training in the steeple was the next logical step so Spike took to spending time with Matilda and coming to terms with the height factor. He discussed the catapult effect on his jump with Gerard Du and concluded that a strong southwest wind was essential to clear the front of the North Transept. This should have started a bout of severe whisker quivering but a healthy mind led to clarity of thought and decision making.

Victor had watched many landings and take-offs of the fliegermaus flights in every sort of weather condition. This, combined with his fastidious note taking in the Daily Diptych regarding details of the loads they were carrying, gave him the insight to brief Spike on what actually happened when a body was projected into space. Victor's time spent in the steeple proved invaluable as did his extensive knowledge of weather moods and patterns.

There were moments when Spike's strength of character did take a nose-dive and it set his whiskers nervously aquivering. But just sitting somewhere quiet, taking deep breaths and thinking of the joy Angelica would feel having her debts settled, seemed to calm him down.

Despite all this though it took all his self-control to live with, and accept, the nagging feeling that he would descend with the velocity of a soft turd dropping into a Ming Vase from a great height.

And to cover roughly the same area on impact!

Matilda had finally reached the level of constructive completion so the fine-tuning could now begin. An Examiner from Health & Safety tested the throwing arm, then proof stamped the leading edge, and it would hereafter need a permit if sold abroad.

There were problems with the ejection seat so an R & D testing base was set up. The prototype hung from a tree and a sack, roughly Spike's weight and volume, was strapped into the seat. Initially the safety catch, when switched to the *Fire* mode, set off the main trigger but this was rectified by increasing the length of wattle tension spring.

The seat angle at the throwing arm's ejecting position was the next hiccup requiring adjustment to the maximum elevation. The ejection point had to be re-positioned as the calculations on the old drawings were for hurling rocks over castle walls and Spike's head might well have been splattered over the ceiling's head in the original design.

And finally the seat profile had to ensure a smooth lift off as any snagging could mean disaster. Nothing was left to chance with a double treble checking before the seat was strapped to TCs back, transported up to the launch pad, and affixed to the throwing arm.

An event date, which could be confirmed when all else had fallen into place, now became dependent on the weather. The correct wind direction was essential with a fine dry day ensuring maximum audience participation, and various traders indicated an interest in setting up stalls on the day so placing the committee in something of a quandary.

It was the middle of Lent and everyone was supposed to give up something.

After much deliberation, coupled with a little bending of the rules, it was agreed that the Church would claim 10% of the traders' take and 25% of the contents of the spectators' purses. On hearing this MacDowell quickly booked a spot outside the Main Gate to set up an Off-Course Betting Stand to access the punters purse before the gatekeepers got their grubby hands on them. Incidentally a late surge on Spike surviving shortened the odds with the bet of chickening out and no-show lengthening to one hundred to one.

The Soothsayers consulted Mother Nature, the Fieldmice were spoken to at length, and the old Sailormice plied with copious quantities of ale in an effort to obtain data for a consolidated informed guess on what one could expect from the weather over the next few weeks. It was finally Victor's arthritis that decided the date – he felt twinges in his back that an itinerant gypsy lady-mouse interpreted as favouring the 31st of March 1529.

Johanne informed Ole that the acclimatisation of his violin, an early Lira da Braccio, had gone according to plan and requested that a rehearsal be arranged for the following Thursday. This was deemed convenient and the group assembled in the late afternoon of the due date.

The candles were turned down with the mice barely able to see the ends of their whiskers but they began to tune their instruments and waited for Johanne to arrive.

None of those present had ever seen a fliegermaus up close but they had all heard dreadful stories of respectable citizenmice, whilst walking about their normal everyday business, being scooped up from above and never seen again. The Flight in residence at the moment was well behaved but the cannibalistic activities of a renegade Flight led by one, Hannibal Nectar, was a frequent leading feature in the Churchmouse Times.

They waited with a mixture of anticipation and excitement.

At the sound of a squeaking handle they turned collectively towards the side door. A tall figure, framed in the doorway by the late evening light, began to materialize.

It disappeared as the door was quietly shut.

Footstep sounds walked down the aisle, stopped, and the *'mouse neckhair standing up on end silence'* was then broken by;

'Guten Abend, wie geht es Ihnen?'

His wingspan seemed to stretch forever so TC moved up to the 2nd position.

Johanne thanked him.

The cat moved back again but was assured that once the wingjoints were fixed, at the correct playing angle, then the fliegermaus would take up very little room.

The rehearsal began and the few spectators, who could see very little in the gloom, were mesmerised by the superb quality of playing and the spectacle of a fliegermaus in full musical accord. The sheer magic of the strings bound the other instruments as one.

'Taking up very little room' seemed at odds with the amount of space Johanne actually needed as his cloak, a FliegerMaus Mk 2 Issue in leather, had a skirt to cover the wings when folded that doubled as a storm flap for use in bad flying weather. An array of straps kept the material in place and several external pockets contained essential bits and bobs. These included a folding crowbar, and a handy-billy to release his comrades whose joints had seized up in the upside down position during their winter hibernation.

TC's flute was knocked out of his mouth and Reggie got the bow in his ear so everyone stood well back to give Johanne the space he actually needed whilst playing. The rehearsal ended on a standing ovation and, together with the spectators, they moved out into the dusk with many questions waiting to be unleashed on an unprepared fliegermaus.

But they had no chance.

He bade them all 'Gute Nacht' and walked quickly away into the darkness.

They felt disappointed but the air abounded with the buzz of musical satisfaction and the magic of his playing would be long remembered.

Next morning Angelica sat in the workroom checking every seam of the parachute with loving care so it was repaired and strengthened where needed. Several of the Town Guilds approached her about displaying their logo on the parachute canopy and this reassured them as big names would not want to be associated with a disaster.

A fast food outlet, opening shortly in town, asked Angelica if they could sponsor a patch on the jump suit. She approached Gerard with this idea and both realized that neither had any idea what Spike planned to wear. They eventually found him in the Scriptorium, his feet up on a stool, and studying the list of things to be done which seemed to be getting longer by the hour.

He looked up as they approached.

'No. No. No way Jose!'

Gerard assured him that it would cut down the wind resistance by half and Angelica would take care of the shaving and trimming.

They were discussing Spike's jumping outfit on the day and his reaction to the suggestion that he shave his legs and trim his whiskers was most adamant. He fidgeted uncomfortably and, when a bead of sweat formed on his upper lip, he took several deep breaths before stretching his quads and sitting down again.

'I planned to wear jogging gear, thick socks, boots and my cloak with an extra cord tied around the knees.'

Gerard could feel the onslaught of a Gallic splutter but managed to cover it with a swiftly applied Size 13. He recovered enough to explain that an arrow flies true to a target because of the streamlining and rarely does it end up elsewhere.

'And if you wear that outfit then I can guarantee you will end up elsewhere bloody well dead at the point of impact.'

Angelica started to sniffle, she had not heard Gerard use strong language before, and the statement gained Spike's attention too. It was finally decided that the jogging top and bottoms, together with the thick socks and boots, could be worn but they needed to find a warm overall to cover everything and give a streamline effect.

She said she would have a look in the Cistercian Op Shop and admitted that she had been quite looking forward to shaving Spike's legs!

Word reached him that a parcel awaited him in the office so Spike made his way over to collect it.

'It must be from home,' he thought and wondered if it contained some of his Mother's home made cake. On arrival Ole, definitely unsteady on his feet, was leaning against the door taking deep gulps of air and making frantic hand signals. Before he realised what was going on Spike had walked right into a toxic cloud of the vilest smelling gas that permeated the eyes, ears, nose and throat.

'God almighty,' he choked, 'what in heaven's name is that?'

'The parcel that came for you,' Ole wheezed in reply. 'It's in the back dustbin.'

His first thought was that his Mother had put in some *'Bleute'* cheese and it had escaped creating havoc amongst the rest of the contents. Eventually however a gust of wind caused the aroma to subside somewhat with his eyes ceasing to water and an improvement in his hearing. It was not until Ole remarked of his failure to understand why anyone in their right mind would send such a vile thing down from the steeple, without cleaning it first, that Spike realised he had somehow lost the plot.

He asked Ole, who was having a good cough, what was in the parcel and he replied that Johanne had sent him down one of the leather flying suits containing something that had swiftly polluted the surroundings.

Reggie arrived with his cart, on to which they lifted the dustbin, and trundled it along to a fast flowing part of the river. Standing well up wind while keeping a firm grip on the cart and the dustbin, Reggie tied one end of a length of cord to the cart handle, the other around the leg of the flying suit, and hooked the offending object out of the bin.

It hit the water with a loud splash and the cart, the dustbin, and both the mice, came within a whisker's width of taking an unscheduled trip downstream to Christchurch.

The riptide continued pulling on the cord but, by adjusting the position of the cart and the length of the rope, the flying suit benefited from a double swirl combining with a tumbling action that cleansed every last morsel of whatever from its interior.

The two mice observed this phenomenon and pondered whether they could patent this cleansing action for tub-washing in generations to come but that train of thought was lost when the cart started to move off position and had to be secured yet again.

It was getting dark when, with the tide on the turn, they pulled the cord in quite easily until the load was ready to be lifted out of the water. Then they struggled and puffed and it was providence that TC arrived, to help lift the suit on to the cart after which they wheeled it to the lavatorium.

Angelica had filled a deep tub with warm water, to which had been added a medley of herbs for restoring the leather, and a few more for luck plus a drop of her own special perfume. Several dead fish fell out of the pockets before the suit was steeped so these were given to the cat who took them home for a late night snack.

Ole had seen Victor, earlier that evening, and asked the reason for the dreadful smell in the flying suit. Evidently one of the fliegermaus had died in his sleep just after the start of the hibernation season and no one had noticed until the wake-up call. Parts of the deceased must have been left behind in the suit but there was no way Ole could mention it to Spike. He put the matter out of his mind, with so many more important things to attend to, and continued with his list for the next morning's meeting.

The churchmice waited in the canteen as Ole had called a special meeting with everyone ordered to attend and the old mouse eventually arrived then sat and caught his breath.

'My Friends, I have several points to make today so please pay attention.'

He put on his glasses and carried on.

'The first is that the Pope is on the mend so we all wish him well.

The second is news of Brother Spikus being granted a full working visa and he can now sleep a tad sounder at nights.'

He nodded in Spike's direction.

'The third point is my pride in the way everyone has helped these last few weeks leading up to the Event.

The fourth point is that Curate Lopes of St Thomas' Church has been officially declared deceased. God rest his soul.

The fifth point is regarding the Service of Thanksgiving for Angelica which will now be combined with one for Brother Spikus after Saturday's Event.'

He nodded and smiled, sort of reassuringly, at Spike.

'And the last and final point is that I have put my resignation before the Cathedral Board which will take effect from St Michalmouse Day.'

With that he stood up, put his glasses in their case, and walked slowly out of the canteen door. Ole was way past retirement age but the suddenness of the news brought a stunned silence, and much communal sadness, to the staff.

Spike left the meeting and walked over to his favourite spot where he sat on the grass in the early spring sunshine. He shook a few crumbs from his pocket for the birds and pondered the points of Ole's speech.

The details of Lopes' demise he tried to shut out as starving to death beneath the Bell Tower was a horrible way to die but that was only speculation. Ole's confirmed date of departure from the Cathedral scene was not far away and the old mouse had looked so tired recently that he deserved the peace of his golden years.

Spike wondered who they had in mind for his replacement.

He blinked back the tears and stood up to brush the grass from his cloak. The midday chimes rang from the Bell Tower as he walked through carpets of daffodils stretching as far as the eye could see.

He felt at peace with the world.

'Stuff the healthy option; I want to eat something I can get my teeth into!'

And with that thought hanging in the air he walked briskly over to the canteen.

Epistle Eight

The Way-up

L anding on the grass posed no problems as he could jump from heights and land running on the spot which was far more difficult than it sounded. During static jumps and dangling from a tree branch he learnt the rules of direction control and emergency untangling of the cords and was even instructed, in the event of landing on someone, just to give his name and roll number. No way was he to apologise or discuss where the fault lay.

Gerard even tried to duplicate wind conditions with a pair of bellows but the combined muscle power of the handymice failed to raise the air velocity to more than a gentle breeze.

It was the final rehearsal on the day before the jump and Reggie had been assigned as a personal bodyguard. Some pretty unsavoury characters had laid out early money, betting on the certainty that the mouse would chicken out, and a nobbling attempt, or worse, might be made before the off.

Spike sat in the ejection seat and, by keeping his elbows well in, could feel the parachute snuggling under his left arm. This was his first time wearing the flying suit and the trouble lay with the pleated covers acting as storm flap. These covered the fliegermaus' wings in bad weather and, although neatly folded with stud fastenings, still caused an extra wide bulk. They should have been removed but, as the suit was only on loan, Spike felt that he couldn't hack great chunks out of it. The side rails had been adjusted to the maximum width but there was still a real risk of the suit snagging so the handymice worked throughout the night fitting a distance piece which, hopefully, would suffice.

The Jump was timed to commence at noon with the gates opening two hours before. Spike slept surprisingly well though he had to get up several times in the night to turn Reggie who was snoring loudly. No attempt at 'nobbling skullduggery' so far had emerged but the hour was early when he started his run and Reggie sat on the grass keeping his friend in sight.

MacDowell, desperate for someone to take on the job of bodyguard, let it be known that only those with reflexes honed to perfection would be considered. Reggie was quite proud to have been selected but he now sat, looking at his own potbelly, to wonder if the local cattle market would class him as 'Prime'.

He stretched his arms but his intention to lean back, only for a moment mind you, was rudely interrupted by a cry and he was on his feet and running towards a scene where Spike was struggling with two black robed figures.

Reggie, drawing back for a full effect, hit the nearest one with a double fisted swing that propelled the offender headfirst into the Close wall then turned to help his friend.

But there was no need! The situation was being handled admirably as Spike landed the first punch. This surge of violence, from our normally friendly churchmouse, stemmed from the recognition of his opponent who happened to be Fat George of the Austins and the sensation of sinking his fist into that fat nose was just the tonic he needed.

The CathCats were quickly summoned to chain the battered and bloodied black canonmice together and drag them away in the direction of the lock-up.

'*To help with their enquiries*'.

An eye cut was seeping blood down Spike's face and every bone in his hand felt broken. Prudence, on duty in the canteen, had recently passed the Health and Safety Examination and knew exactly what to do. The handymice went to fetch Margaret while the hand was plunged into a bowl of ice-cold water and the cut was sprinkled with salt.

Then, opening up the Exouris Accident Diptych, Prudence filled in the details of the incident while still fresh in the patient's mind.

'The parachute is on the left side so it won't make any difference.'

Spike addressed concerns over his damaged hand as Victor relayed news from above that conditions were perfect although the wind might come north-about after lunch.

Margaret thought he should rest for a few days, Ole said it was his own decision and, although the heavily bandaged hand hurt like hell, Spike felt spiritually and physically ready.

Reggie finally tipped the scales by threatening to go in his place so the jump was on.

Essential mousennel only were allowed on the launch pad so the aisle leading to the steeple was lined with well-wishers. Angelica could not stop sobbing but managed to wrap a red woolly scarf, which she had spent hours knitting, around Spike's neck and gave him a good luck kiss. Lisa followed suit but tried to slip her tongue down his throat while Ole gave him a hug. Margaret hung a charm cross around his neck engraved *Jesus Nazarenes Rex* which, he learnt later, was the motto to protect the wearer against sudden death!

TC sat waiting and Spike, with tears rolling down his cheeks, gave a final wave before climbing onto the cat's back to commence the long journey up to the steeplecross.

The Launchpad

At every landing TC went into the pause mode to catch his breath and regain his balance as Ole had given him instructions that the mouse's energy had to be maintained at all costs and if that meant knackering the cat so be it.

Their relief, however, on reaching the launch pad, was evident but if they expected someone to be on hand when they stepped on to the floor then they were disappointed. The cat, although he'd promised to hang about for as long as was necessary, wasn't really fond of heights and suffered from the *twitchy bottom syndrome*! The mouse noticed the symptoms and asked TC to leave, quite kindly actually, but then the tears started to flow and dealing with a loud, obviously distressed cat wasn't on Spike's list of *'Important things to do immediately prior to the jump'*.

Then Victor, on hearing the sobbing, shouted up from somewhere below; '*For God's sake get shot of that bleeden cat!*' TC gave a loud sniff, wished Spike all the luck in the world, and started down the steps promising that they would meet up after the jump.

And, as he watched the cat descend, Spike wondered if they ever would.

Matilda sat quietly gleaming at the entrance and, to prevent any unspecified departures ahead of time, the safety net stretched over the doorway. His flying suit and parachute lay folded on the bench with the socks and boots tucked neatly underneath.

In the corner a D.I.Y. chapel had been set up with a simple cross and a lighted candle together with an aspergillum in a stoup of holy water and one level below the launch pad party was still in conference so he leaned against the net and breathed deeply.

And looked down.

The crowds, just one black mass, covered the Close and the Wiltshire countryside seemed to stretch away forever. With a wind direction favouring a path away from the North Transept, he wondered how far he would drift. Just then the sun broke through so, after a few more deep breaths, he crossed the floor to the chapel in the corner.

In an attempt to share these precious, and maybe his last, moments with family and friends he knelt and cupped his good hand over the flame. Their faces, pictured in his mind's eye, dissolved into one mirage and a wet-eye started of its own accord. His life was in the hands of The Creator who, at the right time, would decide whether to give the thumbs up or down.

One of Gerard Du's size 13s came to the rescue and, after a good nose blow, he felt much better and was appreciative of the time alone.

He felt no fear, just an incredible loneliness which brought with it an inner peace.

'No one to help me now,' he stated to the empty landing.

The peace and solitude were soon shattered however by the half-hour strike from the Bell Tower that rattled the fillings in his teeth. The chimes would be silenced prior to the Noonshot in case the vibrations affected Matilda.

'Nearly ready then son?'

Victor's voice broke the impasse as he, followed by Gerard and the handymice, climbed up on to the launch pad.

'As ready as I will ever be,' replied Spike who failed miserably at his attempt to put on a brave smile. Victor and Gerard, each with their own checklist, seemed to be working much better together and the reasons for this were twofold.

An aura of calm had to be around the launch pad as any flare-up could adversely affect Spike's peace of mind and Ole had threatened to lock them both up in chains, in the Bell Tower cellars, on bread and water, if our hero was upset in any way what-so-ever!

Gerard locked the trigger catch in safe mode as Spike wound Angelica's scarf around his neck and was helped into his flying suit by the handymice. They fitted the parachute harness and lifted Spike up into the throwing arm seat of Matilda. With one leg either side of the crosstree, the Q.R. clips were set to automatically release when the seat had reached the throwing arm's high point. And he would then be clear, according to the instructions, '*to fling the canopy upwards*' and '*float gently down to earth*'.

He chewed constantly on wads of dropwort and willow to relieve the pain and the throbbing up his arm, together with the bulk of the flying suit, made sitting even more uncomfortable. The canopy, tucked under his left arm, needed to be freed by his one good hand so it was therefore essential that his other hand be unrestricted to clear any tangles.

And a bandaged hand would be worse than useless.

'Here, take a good swig of this.'

Spike could feel the liquid burning a path down his throat as Gerard unwrapped the bandages.

It was from a flask of Victor's '*King Alfred's Navy Rum*', distilled in the steeple, and which only saw the light of day on very special occasions.

The last time was the signing of the Anglo-Scots peace in 1526.

He took another swig from the flask, remembering Uncle Zeb relating tales of the Italian Campaign, and a couple of his sayings came to mind.

'Always plenty of rum to drink before you went over the top lad,' which was always followed by; 'And courage is fear holding on a moment longer,'.

'That's how I feel,' said Spike to no one in particular, 'like I'm going over the top.'

'Mein Gott.' Gerard exclaimed, straying slightly from his native tongue as he released the bandages to unveil a multi coloured swollen mitt.

'You can't jump with a hand like that.'

Another swig gurgled down Spike's throat

'I am here and I am going to jump,' came the reply, 'with or without your help.'

Then, draining the last of the dregs from the flask, he wiped his mouth with the back of his bad hand and stated; 'So let's get on with it.'

Victor produced a second flask and, as they toasted Spike's good health, Gerard started to say that Chartres would have put on only the very best champagne for such an occasion but Victor eyeballed him so the statement quickly terminated into a size 13.

Two moments by the sun dial gear wheel remained on the board.

Spike got hold of the flask again and started to sing an Old Italian love song which brought tears to everyone's eyes. He then proposed a toast to all Mothers wherever they may be, before letting out a loud fart and asking to go to the loo.

The launch party tactically ignored his request, while liberally spraying the surrounds with killpong, as Victor had checked the wind direction and noted it was swiftly coming around to the north sooner than expected.

They had to go now so Gerard started the countdown as the handymice rolled up the net.

'Ten /nine /eight /seven /six /five /four /three /two.'

The chocks were quickly cleared and the weights released.

'One.'

Victor moved to the trigger, eased back the safety catch intending to give a quick *'God be with you'* thumbs up blessing, but saw to his horror that Spike had dropped off to sleep clutching the flask and was starting to snore.

He paused, thought, then decided and his finger pulled, albeit reluctantly, the trigger.

The Waydown

He was dreaming.

He must be dreaming.

He felt so cold and seemed to be floating.

Not floating but falling and the sun rolled around the sky.

'Holy Jesus!'

What other expression could a fast falling mouse use?

The crosstree had come off in his hands and, with half the canopy wrapped around it, all the cords were knotted awkwardly under one shoulder. He tried to re-position himself but the lines became even more firmly tangled and both his hands were starting to freeze up.

'I don't want to die, God don't let me die.'

These anguished cries were lost in the noise of the airstream as he plummeted towards the earth. If only he could clear the cords but there was nothing left to do. Our hero's options had run out with only a few moments or so before the big 'KERPLOP'.

He shut his eyes tight and hoped for the best. What else was a fast falling mouse all tangled up in his parachute expected to do?

Meanwhile up in the heavens 'The Creator' opened the book and sharpened his quill in anticipation

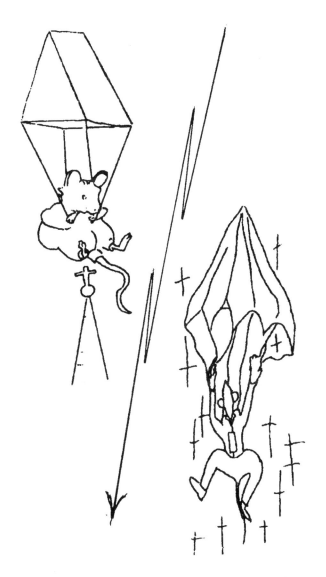

The Idea & Reality were, in a flash, torn assunder.

of entering the name of yet another hardy soul who thought he could fly like a bird.

'Offen zee klips.'

Spike thought he heard a voice and opened one eye.

Something ornithological, huge and black, blotted out the light.

'This is all I need,' he muttered convinced that the Archangelmouse of Death, St Tarquin, had arrived to take down his particulars.

'Offen zee bliddy klips.'

'What clips?'

It crossed his mind that he was talking to God.

'Zee bliddy ving flieganzee klips.'

He then realised it was Johanne Maus hovering around his upper quarter.

'Zee ving klips. Unter zee bliddy arms.'

Spike reached across and managed to release one.

The nearside wing cover caught the airstream and he found himself doing a figure of eight with a cheer going up from the crowd below who were most impressed by this show of airmouseship. He pulled at the other clip, with his bad hand, but any reserves of strength had ebbed away and the pain of the effort nearly made him pass out.

The clip held tight as his direction suddenly changed and he started to corkscrew downwards, very fast, towards the looming flying buttresses.

At that point he felt a strong yank on his left side after which the lights went out.

Johanne, dipping into one of his many pockets, had extended the Mk 2 scissored arm and, hovering dangerously close to a lee wind target, managed to hook onto the clip.

This latest development, which quickly ballooned the other wing cover, arrested his ground bound direction to send him eastwards as the northwest wind caught the cover. He soared around the North Transept and over the Morning Chapel where he gained a little height before passing out of sight behind the Bishop's Palace.

Missing believed lost

They waited for him to appear.

The Handymice Runners would be returning soon with our hero mouse carried shoulder high.

A sigh of collective relief rose from the assembled crowd.

He had been found but with head injuries.

The crowd fell silent.

He had been found but dead.

Collective relief was replaced by collective grief.

Pieces of parachute material quickly appeared on the vender's stalls.

'Martyred? Of course he will be martyred. Look at this Sir, still warm.'

'Genuine and gently separated from the body only a few moments ago.'

And so it went on.

'Here Madam, this one has bloodstains so buy now this never to be repeated offer.'

'Last pieces of the shroud from the body of a Martyr which clothed the bruised and battered body not a few minutes ago. Would my lovely wife lie?'

Meanwhile, in the vestry, Ole voiced his concerns to a somewhat bewildered team as he had only catered for one of two scenarios.

The death scenario had the funereal detail, selected from the tallest of the handymice suitably attired in black cloaks and tall hats, ready to tactfully retrieve the remains of our fallen hero in a dignified and sombre manner. A pair of laying out boards had been fixed together, side by side, just in case Spike had spread himself, albeit thinly, over a larger area of the Close.

The survival scenario was that he be hoisted, shoulder high, and carried by a team of gaily-dressed handymice, complete with bells on their fingers and toes, right into the Cathedral. Ole had not asked Mr Knyght's permission but reckoned he could get away with such a blatant disregard of the Cathedral's sanctuary during the initial euphoria and celebration.

And any flak would be sorted after the event.

However Spike, disappearing somewhere into the middle distance, was an event which took Ole a little time to get his head around.

'We must find him, where is he?'

'Get anyone from St Thomas' and St Martin's only do something.'

His team started to run in many different directions at the same time in their attempt to 'do something'!

'I can't bother with that now. Lock him up somewhere.'

Ole was referring to Victor, tied to a pole and being carried about by handymice who were wondering what on earth to do with him.

The old mouse, convinced that he was the cause of Spike's death, had tried to space-walk from the steeple as a penance and had planned to go when Gerard's attention was elsewhere.

Edging towards the door, ready for the off, it was only when he went on and on asking forgiveness from a list of saints as long as your arm that Gerard had turned around to find out what was going on. He only had time to grab a leg, the rest being halfway out the door, and had then managed to drag Victor back inside before lashing him to Matilda.

A rising Evening Star signalled the crowd that the day was done so the vendors closed up with the parachute remnants all but sold out. This 'nice little earner' had started life early in the day as a damaged bed-linen joblot from Solly the Jew.

MacDowell had a near riot on his hands when he refused to pay out on anything until Spike had been found, either dead or alive, or officially declared missing presumed lost by the church. His foresight in inviting a few of his Glasgow Hardmice friends to help out saved him from being lynched. The crowds were hostile with some convinced Spike was dead, while others said that the jump had been completed, so a fight breaking out between them gave MacDowell the chance to escape showing, to the surprise of his friends, quite a nifty pair of heels.

Every creature associated with the church was on the prowl searching high and low, in and out, up and down and round and round.

They tried different combinations.

Up and round, high and out, in and down, low and round but all to no avail.

By dawn the foot parties had reported back and The Fliegermaus Flight, airborne and searching in grid pattern formation all night, touched down absolutely exhausted. Johanne, still badly traumatised from his midday exposure, relayed the news to Ole.

'No trace.'

Spike had disappeared from the immediate area so messengers were sent to Mudeford, and other coastal ports, carrying an all points bulletin for the fishing fleet;

'Please keep an eye open for a solo flying mouse possibly heading over the Channel towards France.'

Ole took charge of the situation and stood everyone, except essential staff, down for the day and the mess in the grounds stayed on the ground.

He told his weary troops that they had done well but could do no more as Spike's salvation now lay firmly in the lap of the Gods.

Tolitha, Early April 1529

She twisted her hanky as the chimes struck seven leaving her wondering what had happened to her Charlie. He was Potts' replacement and, after their meeting on the first day, it was love at first sight.

'He must have worked late, that's what it is.'

A small parliament of rooks, scratching on the grass for an evening snack, nodded in agreement. The huge clean up, started at first light, now had the surrounds of the Bishop's Palace looking spruce and tidy although the smoke hung heavy in the evening air from the piles of torched rubbish.

Tolitha looked up into the sky and remembered the brave mouse, who had zoomed over that very spot all tangled up in his parachute before, apparently, sprouting wings. She was most impressed by the fine display of airmouseship and watched in amazement as he sort of 'aerocartwheeled' away in the distance.

'Poor little darling,' she said and gave an involuntary shiver.

Charlie arrived at that very moment to take advantage of the shiver and the pair tippy toed down the stairs into the laundry.

'Ohhhh.'

'What on earth was that?' asked Charlie as his passion started to wane.

'Just the wind my darling,' she replied undoing one side of the rear support cordage on her drawers and starting on the other.

'Ohhhh.'

Charlie's passion, now in freefall, propelled him up the steps and out leaving poor Tolitha struggling desperately to reverse the cordage support situation in her drawers.

'Who's there?'

The question came out as a defiant challenge before the Maid finished doing herself up and edged towards the stairs intent on finding her Charlie.

Ascending the stairs, two at a time, she finally caught up with him but only had time for a quick kiss before he went as his main concern seemed to be the *'Ghost of the Laundry Room'*.

Tolitha, up at the crack of dawn, unlocked the chute door and pulled it open. It was dirty laundry sort day and she had many baskets to fill before Charlie collected them after lunch.

She clipped the door secure and had just started to descend when she heard something.

'Ohhhh.'

'There it is again,' she said to herself, 'it must be the wind.'

Her boot caught the corner of what looked like a fine dustsheet lying by one pile and, noticing that it was attached to a cord, she pulled.

Out slid slowly, from beneath the linen, a fliegermaus shaped leatherclothed figure with hardly enough strength to raise a smile.

She gave a jump and then a scream.

Spike tried to stand but couldn't.

'Could you get me water and assistance; I think my leg is broken.'

Remembering her NVQ safety training, especially the part which stated;

'Do not give food or drink to an injured person. Do not try to move them and seek medical help immediately.'

Tolitha assumed the rules applied to an injured mouse so, as with the previous evening, she took the steps two at a time and ran out onto the grass.

Reggie, jogging along the East Wall, saw the Maid waving her arms and changed direction towards her.

'The flying mouse, Brother Spikus, down in the laundry cellar.'

His feet didn't miss a beat and followed her down the steps where Spike was trying to undo the parachute.

'Saints in heaven you're safe, we thought you were brown bread.'

'Give me some water for God's sake.'

Three full ladles were emptied before Spike finally shook his head.

'Get this bloody parachute off me; I think my leg is broken.'

Reggie undid the straps and wrapped up the chute in the cords.

'See if you can fix these wing flaps in place.'

She gently lifted him and managed to fix the flaps but Spike had lost consciousness by this time so the three of them quickly made their way to the canteen where Tolitha laid the mouse onto a tabletop before leaving as she still had mountains of laundry to sort through.

Reggie summoned the duty handymice, who were luckily in the canteen but unlucky to be only halfway through their Full English Breakfast, and they carried their unconscious precious load back through the side door and into the canteen where Angelica, busy cooking cheese scones, worked on completely unaware of the drama about to unfold.

She turned to the sight of Spike being carried past her workbench and first she screamed, then fell down, stood up, and finally fainted.

Reggie shook her and she opened her eyes.

'The laying out board, why bring him here?'

'It's a table top, not the laying out board, and he's O.K,' Reggie assured her but she had fainted again so Reggie left her to it; he never did quite understand the female species.

Margaret arrived breathless at the canteen with Prudence in tow. The news had been flashed around like bushfire and the churchmouse medical team responded with their usual dedication.

'Knife.'

One was quickly produced and the leg cover of the flying suit slit from ankle to waist with the jogging bottoms being similarly treated. The broken limb, after being strapped to a splint, was supported as the mouse was lifted clear of the suit.

The leg was inspected, cleaned and set.

A liberal application of soothing balmweed was followed by a triple splint before a cover of clean hempcloth, soaked in a mixture of crushed chalk and water, was allowed to set hard. Finally a dressing of dockleaf salve, in a soft bandage, was wrapped around his swollen hand.

And Spike muttered and snored through the whole operation, as did Angelica who had been lifted onto one of the chairs.

Meanwhile Ole, who just happened to be passing, explained that Spike must have completed a left-hand vertical turn behind the Bishop's Palace before disappearing into the laundry chute. The delivery later that day must have pushed him further down, and under the linen pile, so after Tolitha had shut the doors no one thought of looking down there.

Why should they?

But the important thing was that our mouse was safe and well and he was carried, still fast asleep, back to his cell and his own bunk.

And clutched in his hot little hand was a sick note, signed by 'Sister Carbolic', for one month's complete bed rest!

Epistle Nine

The Price of Fame

Sitting up in bed and draining the last dregs of a delicious bowl of potato and leek soup, Spike licked his lips and reflected on the events of the last week.

Media interest had been fast tracked owing to the newly appointed air correspondent of the Churchmouse Times using phrases like *'Return from the Dead'* and other eye catching headlines. This attracted every form of local life into the Close with a desire to see the hero mouse and shake him by his good hand while dissatisfied punters, those who had lost their shirts mousesize or otherwise, still wanted to check that our hero was really alive.

The crowds on that first day greeted the news of Spike's safe return with joy and relief with enormouse numbers assembling in the Close but by nightfall the CathCats were in danger of losing control so Ole ordered that Spike be moved to more secure accommodation.

He was smuggled into the Cat Compound under the cover of darkness and TC was then delegated the responsibility for Spike's safety. Old Harry later had a quiet word in TC's shell-like which, roughly translated, read; 'Don't cock this one up else yer on yer bike.'

Spindrift was covering a family bereavement at Christchurch Priory so Spike was installed in his room. The decor was very striking, blending earthy coloured walls and a blue ceiling with a neutral floor co-coordinating the pastel drapes and scatter cushions.

It was so tranquil and the ambience definitely speeded up the healing process.

With the aid of a crutch he could now hop to the toilet and even sit outside on warm mornings to exercise his hand. One of the early problems however was the food as the staple diet produced in the Cat Compound kitchen was fish and Spike had always found fish difficult to digest. At the end of the first day he suffered a stomach upset requiring numerous trips to the loo and TC decided it was the *'Bloater a la King with Wild Rice'* served up for lunch.

By the end of the next day however he must have tasted so many types of herring that the only one he hadn't tried was a red one so, in answer to Margaret's request during her early morning round of *'Any complaints'*, Spike had a good whinge about the food.

Ole heard about it and spoke to Angelica who created wonderful examples of mouse cuisine especially designed to titillate the tastebuds of the patient. Even Lisa produced mousewatering cakes and biscuits from the kitchen of her Auntie Vi who lived nearby and the competition between the two ladymice sometimes led to sharp words and scurrilous rumours.

Consternation naturally arose amongst other staff members regarding the standard menu to which

Angelica lent a sympathetic ear before indicating the direction of the nearest dustbin.

If either of the ladymice delivered the meals they would climb into bed with him on the pretence of supporting his leg whilst he ate. The bed, being cat size with lots of room, led to Lisa and her gang arriving one evening when they all got into bed with him.

TC arrived in the middle of all this and, much to his embarrassment, didn't know where to put his face.

Lisa had a suggestion that made him even more embarrassed!

Salisbury Market Day on that particular Saturday was no place for an injured mouse to be hobbling around on a crutch. A quiet afternoon stroll meandering along the river bank in the spring sunshine, with Angelica and regular rest stops, sounded very agreeable until they happened to bump into Lisa on the Main Path.

The gentle stroll then became a Market stroll-laround stroll.

Spike went along reluctantly as, what with a leg still in plaster and a crutch in use, frequent sit-downs were needed. It was uncomfortable keeping his hood up whilst wearing shades but this was essential as, being Mouse of the Moment, a snippet from anywhere, body or dress, was in great demand especially amongst the local ladymice.

Only last week Angelica had to slap the face of some strumpetmouse who put her hand inside of Spike's cloak on the pretence that her foot had slipped and she'd grabbed the nearest upright for support!

The first call was at Mabel's *'Cartwheel Buttons from Blandford'* stall, where Angelica had to pick up a couple of cards, before arriving at the *'Chez DameMaus Dress'* where the two ladymice were soon caught up in a frenzy of trying on this and that.

Spike's opinion was initially sought but, as usual in these situations, he quickly became surplus to requirements. He asked the stallholdingmouse if there was somewhere to sit, as his good leg was starting to ache, and he was surprised to be led by the arm to a seat in the changing room where different ladymice were in various stages of undress.

Some of them were very tasty indeed and no one took the slightest notice of him. They just carried on, taking their gear off and trying on various dresses, as if he wasn't there. With his hood up, shades and a crutch, he quickly realised they thought he was a blind cripple so, leaving his shades on, he sat back to enjoy this unexpected bonus.

They must have thought him deaf as well as blind because the language left a lot to be desired with the opinions of some partners very scathing. After a while his stomach started to rumble as hunger dictated it was time for tea so, positioning his crutch for a straight lift, he was interrupted by a familiar voice ringing out.

'Hello Spike, what are you doing here?'

It was Margaret standing there with a dress over her arm and a gleam in her eye.

'Just resting my leg...'

The reply carried no conviction whatsoever.

'Don't let me disturb you then...' And she proceeded to strip quickly and provocatively down to her nether garments, and beyond, with her eyes not leaving his for a moment.

She tried on the dress.

'See you around then, I have found what I want…' And then she was gone.

He didn't need a crutch to remove himself from the immediate area and he made his weary way back to the Cathedral. His slow path was comforted with some interesting thoughts about Margaret, who'd had quite a reasonable body, and wondering if Angelica and Lisa had been picked up by some sailormice and taken on board the wool barge.

The day had certainly been one to remember!

Ole, Late April 1529

St Michalmouse`s Day had been earmarked for his retirement so, along with two other retirees, the celebrations would be shared.

Norman, from St Thomas', was handing in his cross as the last few years had been stressful but his replacement, from Durham Cathedral, spoke with an accent so strong that no one could understand him. Erskine therefore, who had a vast experience of far off lands, their inhabitants and weird tongues during his seagoing career, was appointed Cat-in-Charge of St Thomas' and would interpret the Geordie lingo for others. He seemed a nice enough chapmouse though so everyone put in an extra effort and listened very hard.

The third retiree was Victor who, although back to his old self after the suicide attempt, had connections with a well-known group of cheese tasters in Trowbridge. It was suggested that retirement in that area was the only option so an effort was made to find out Victor's true age.

A sister, traced to the office mousehole of St Martins, thought he had been a boymouse at Old Sarum but that would have made him over 250 years old so it was just agreed to list his retirement age as 'very old indeed'!

George and Cedric, the Austin prisoners, were still in chains and traumatised from being locked up for weeks in that awful cellar but when they were due to be handed back to their Mothermouse Chapter, Ole demanded the following conditions;

'The Area Chief Augustinemonkmouse to collect them himself.'

'A written formal apology be offered to Spike and Reggie for the unseemly behaviour of two of his chapter.'

'Angelica's debts to be cleared in full on receipt of a final payment that must be written off in lieu of compensation for a nightstick broken during the cross examination process.'

In return, Spike and Reggie had to sign a declaration that;

'They shalt not abuse, threaten or make faces at any Monkmouse in the future and all past offences be forgiven.'

The Area Chief was furious with Ole who insisted that, unless the apology was given in good grace without the scowl, he could clear off and come back next week. He eventually fulfilled the requests so with their business thereby concluded the Austin group, led by their fuming Chief, were seen off the Cathedral grounds.

It was suggested that the Chief be offered a farewell glass of something.

The Mouse in Charge's reply to that – *'Stuff Em'*.

Ole had been looking tired those last couple of weeks so, during a quiet moment sitting just chatting, Spike suggested that the old mouse went home and put his feet up.

'That's just the trouble, she won't leave me alone.' he muttered and went into some detail regarding Margaret's sudden awakening of passion.

'My wife has been buying all sorts of underwear, far too young for her, and demanding immediate attention on my arrival home. Sometimes before I have had time to take off my cloak or put down the shopping.'

He continued but in a lower tone. 'And she has even suggested that we answer some of those weird adverts on the back of the Churchmouse Times.'

'Still,' he mused, 'after a few glasses of wine she soon drops off to sleep and then I can take advantage of a bit of a lie down too.'

Spike appeared just to listen and nod but his mind was racing off tangentially in all directions.

Spike, Temptation

He stretched it and wiggled his toes before deciding that his leg was well on the mend. The cover had to be removed before the big day so Margaret said she'd call on her way home with the necessary equipment. That morning a walking stick had arrived to replace the crutch and Spike was giving the wood a final polish when there was a soft knock on the cell door.

'Ready for your leg off then?'

She walked in, shutting the door firmly, then took out a large pair of scissors and pulled up a stool.

'Take your cloak off and sit on the bed.'

It was removed and he sat.

'Can you stand on it and is there any pain?'

The answer was yes and no.

'Put your leg on my lap.'

She lent forward to start the cutting action and then, as the top buttons on her coverall came undone, he saw she had nothing underneath and his mind dwelt on Ole's words.

'She wants my attention all the time.'

Thankfully the plaster cover soon came away and she poured a few drops of oil on to her hands. Soft and firm, they massaged his leg working their way slowly up his thigh, and his mind went back to the changing room at 'Chez DameMaus'.

With nether regions starting to stir, seemingly having a mind of their own, he desperately tried concentrating his thoughts on Cherie, the Chief Minister's wife whose face was enough to put anyone off rumpty pumpty for life but all to no avail.

It started to rise to the occasion and nothing he could do, or think of, could stop it.

Margaret must have noticed, even knocking against it a couple of times, but said nothing and then, gently wiping the leg dry of oil, she applied a light bandage and asked if it felt comfortable. 'Lean against me and put some weight on it.'

He did and there were no embarrassing projections so she put the old cover into the bin and told him to use the stick for the next week at least.

'Any trouble with the hand?' she asked putting the scissors into her bag and then, looking down at the bunk, changed the tone from her hospital voice.

'Good Luck for tomorrow. We are all very proud of you.'

And then she was gone leaving Spike quite emotional and tearful.

He sat quietly for a while until he felt better and retrieved the old cover from the bin.

'By hook or by crook I'll be laste on this caste.'

Lisa had written this right at the top so he cut the piece out, propped it up on the shelf, gave his nose a good blow, then walked around the block to test-drive his mended leg before carrying on to the canteen for the evening meal.

Spike, sitting in the sun by the Cat Compound, observed a kafuffle around the Main Gate and initially thought it was a surprise visit by the ArchCardinal Mouse Innocenti XV11. He then spotted a ladymouse, clothed in the latest fashion and topped with a red beret secured with a large hatpin, striding out in front of a column of layabout mice each carrying an item of luggage. When Angelica appeared he realised it was her sister Cheribina who was taking a few days off to attend the Thanksgiving Concert and, according to Angelica, had also read about his exploits in the Eling Echo and was desperate to meet him in person.

Such is the price of fame! The thought crossed his mind as he stretched his arms and lay back in the sun.

Reggie, Early May 1529

His contribution to the concert was to give the correct number of 'bongs' at the right time but Reggie was one worried mouse convinced that he would cock things up. He desperately needed a blow that would relieve frayed nerves hanging together by a fine thread but Ole's orders were specific;

Stay off the grass.

For the last few days Spike had got him up early for jogging practice and today, the day of the concert, was no exception. He sat counting Reggie's circuits on the Green but his mind kept wandering back to the day of the jump.

The steeple looked so high and, pondering how on earth he had plucked up the courage, decided that it was quite an achievement and he felt proud that his name, *'Brother Spikus'*, would be on record forever more and wondered if his Mum had read about it in the local *'Avvisi'*.

His friend came into view looking absolutely knackered and Spike decided that any facetious remarks were best left unsaid. So, with himself at a limp and Reggie at a stagger, they made their weary way to the canteen for a well-earned breakfast.

In charge of the food preparation for the day of the concert was Angelica who made it clear that this was Spike and her's own special time. MacDowell's request to invite some Scottish friends was initially turned down until she discovered that Sean, one of the group, was a fully trained Cordon Bluemouse who offered to help with the fingerfood and dips.

This was tactfully accepted only after she had met this strapping specimen who hailed from the Isle of Skye, wore a kilt of the MacNab tartan, and expertly danced a jig on two lucifers.

And she rather fancied him as well!

Today however the canteen was a scene of chaos with Angelica standing nearby close to tears. The food delivery cart had been stolen during the night which meant that the first lot of contract sandwiches, fetched by hand, arrived with the edges all turned up and droopy in the middle. Reggie offered his bag cart that, while not designed for the carriage of finger-food, could easily be adapted. This offer seemed to revive Angelica so he wheeled the cart over to the washplace and set about cleaning the frame.

A number of spiders and insects, most of whom had been residents of the cart for a number of years, had to be dislodged. Reggie had looked upon these creatures almost as family but insisted that there was a crisis and it only meant them sleeping rough for one night. Their faces fell further however when told to remove all their belongings as anything left behind would be spotted by the eagle eyed Angelica and removed straight into the destructor.

He soon had the cart spotless and, after a final polish, Angelica passed it *'Fit4food'*.

Ole arrived at midday and called the meeting to order. The smallest chapel, the Beauchamp Chantry, had been set aside for the concert and a vent grid removed so Johanne could enter and leave without fuss. He was only too pleased to play but felt unable to handle the huge interest his presence seemed to generate. Flying in from above would cause pandemonium to break out below so he usually landed at a quiet spot nearby and walked the rest.

The order of Service was detailed and Ole mentioned that the choice of music was the prerogative of Angelica and Spike. His personal choice would have been selected pieces more in keeping with the occasion but, noticing his wife glaring from the stalls, hurriedly added that it would all be very enjoyable.

He went on to confirm that the Mic at St Thomas', Brother Yoric, would be succeeding him but advised that his own authority would still be in force for a while albeit in a purely advisory capacity. The efforts of all concerned over the past few months were praised and he concluded with a stern reminder that the celebration party was an opportunity to have a bite to eat, a yarn with friend, and a glass of cheer.

It was not, he emphasised the not, an excuse for a ginourmouse piss-up!

MacDowell, Gerard, Reggie and Spike were individually eyeballed in turn before he gathered up his papers and walked out.

Epistle Ten

The Final Curtain

They all filed over to the canteen where Angelica had laid out soup and toast under a time limit rule meaning the bowls were quickly collected whether they were empty or not. And the orders of the day, apart from clean faces and feet, were best cloaks and highly polished sandals so the mice were soon back in their cells for a quick wash, whisker brush and teeth clean.

Reggie's teeth were rattling a lively calypso as he sat on his bunk while Spike, in an effort to calm his friend's stage nerves, kept feeding him wads of St John's Wort. He was also trying to fit a pair of shades over a rather bulbous nose as Reggie's concentration span seemed to be in direct proportion to the length of Lisa's mini skirt.

Spike thought that a polarised outlook might help keep Reggie's mind on the music!

Mr Knyght welcomed guests at the chapel door and all the seats were quickly occupied leaving standing room only. The level of chatter was noisy and high pitched until Ole swept through the door, resplendent in the scarlet cloak reserved for such special occasions, and ascended the rostrum. His opening speech was thankfully short then he nodded to the performing artists who arose, as one, to file behind the screen where Johanne and TC were waiting in position and all the mousicians, plus one cat, proceeded to tune up their instruments and voices.

MacDowell performed a triple tonguing mid-chord reverse change at the top end of his mouse-organ with Gerard-Du giving a deep melodic interpretation of Spike's high velocotic parachuteless descent towards Mother Earth on his didgeridoo.

These solo tasters were followed by Ole, the Micetro designate, waving his baton around in quite frightening swirls and a spontaneous round of applause followed. It was very impressive but soon the instruments fell silent and the audience hushed their chatter.

Spike, having been appointed Mic of stage, chairs and props, was supposed to swish back the curtain but, not having a 100% balance, was lifted off his feet and swished along in the opposite direction. He failed to let go and felt such a pillock suspended high above the stage. One of the handymice, the strain of trying not to laugh very obvious on his face, had to fetch a ladder to help him down and the curtain eventually swished back as planned.

There was an audible gasp from all as Johanne with TC in one corner, Lisa and the group centre stage, and the rest dotted around turned, in staccato, to face the front.

Ole looked up and tapped his baton sharply.

The opening piece, a Celtic Salisbarium Chant from back-a-long-way-way, involved the gathering forming into one voice and thereby creating the magical ambiance for such an occasion.

This was followed by TC and Johanne duetting, '*A Spring Medley for Flute and Violin*' from opposite ends of the stage, and this had the guests in raptures.

Lisa and her group, in the shortest of skirts, then shimmied on from behind the curtain and started the hands-a-clapping with; '*Tell me what you want what you really really want*' and '*Another one hits the dust*' which brought the proceedings up to the interval.

Ole took to the stage in the second half, first reading the 23rd Psalm from the good book and then enthusiastically conducted his two favourite hymns; '*The Old Rugged Cross*' and '*Abide with me*', that ended with not a dry eye in the place.

Lisa with the group, and looking nothing like a Mother Superior or her nuns, then returned in full costume for their version of; '*Eidelmice*' and ended with an individual splintered key quivering warbling descant rendering of '*Climb every mountain*'.

Reggie, christened for the duration of the Service as '*Him of the Shielded Glance*', was bong perfect throughout and switched on his best smile that lit up the whole chapel.

This triggered off a loud cheer and he hung up his bongos to move centre stage where, with the enthusiastic encouragement from the entertainers and coordinated clapping from the audience, he performed an impromptu soft shoe shuffle that caused the roof of the Beauchamp Chantry to strain at her stays.

Such an outburst of appreciation had been rarely observed in God's house but, on this special occasion, the gathering went absolutely bananas.

Unfortunately the spontaneity of the event was never, sadly ever, heard in the Cathedral again.

Narrator's Note

I am at the Library checking any records of Thanksgiving Services and the man who knows all, there is one in most reference sections, has pointed me in the right direction as on the desk before me are 'The Churchwarden's Accounts of Salisbury Cathedral 1443–1702' published by The Wilts Centennial Record Society.

I look up May 1529, as St Michalmouse Day was on the 19th, and find some entries for the last two weeks of the month;

Paymentys, Fynes and Reparations.
To—Mother Rose for sowying ouer of albys—-iiijd.
From—Granny Spyce whom runneth a dysorderly place entertayning saylors withyn the city walls.—-Fyned iiijd.
To—Thomas Prynce for lb of visitacion light.—-viijd.
To—Kyith Baldrik for diggyng gravyes to fit Mt Strytch and Ms Strytch.—-vijd.
To—Sir Humpfry for money by hym payde to Mr Weuer for kepynge of masses.—-iiijs.
From—Twoah Churchmiice of yon Cathedral, Browther Spikus UM and Black Reggie, for disorderly conduct in Saynt Martin's Chapel. To witt. They doath swingeth on the fayst whyel jumpeth in yon Foynt, and wasteth loo paper. Fyned— iiijd eyach. Bowned o'er to keypp yon pyace.'

There is more oldy worldy writing that I'm unable to read so the man who knows all, I really must ask his real name, translates it for me and this is the gist of what he finds.

192

On Monday, the 21st of May, 1529, two Chapter Churchmice, Brother Spikus U.M. and Black Reggie, were up before the *'Ecclesiastical Beak'* on a charge of causing mayhem in the early hours of Sunday morning at the Church of St Martin by swinging on the fasting wheel and jumping in the font. In the words of Reggie who, when asked by the Vergermouse what on earth he was doing, replied; 'We know how far he can travel in the vertical plane so I'm just checking out his horizontal projectile distance.'

The District Circuitormouse arrived at daybreak to fill out the charge sheet before locking them both up in the coalhole. An additional charge of *'bowling a loo roll',* where the roll was unraveled down the center aisle like the shroud of Christ, was dismissed on a technicality.

'It's a sad state of affairs,' Spike was told, 'to see a U.M. behaving like a hooliganmouse.'

The Beak then advised him to undergo counselling in an effort to halt an early advent of Perdition, the risk of Anathema, and a certain downward spiral into Hades.

They were both fined and bound over to keep the peace.

Following an event of such unusual diversity I also found that some records were struck out from the Cathedral Register during the Civil War. The Service of Thanksgiving could have been amongst them but they missed the charge sheets.

I return to the journal.

Spike, The Ultimate Recognition

The euphoria at that euphonic experience came to its natural conclusion as hands tired and the clapping ceased. Ole, carrying a package tied with a red satin bow, climbed up on to the rostrum.

'Friends.'

He coughed and continued;

'The Brotherhood of Universal Meteorites, literally meaning *'falling bodies'*, has it's roots in Greek antiquity dedicated to the idea of flying like a bird.'

Johanne, standing quietly at the back, was given the nod.

'Certain species already had that ability with man and mouse wanting to be like them. This award, sadly, has always been presented posthumously until today and there were moments quite recently when I was convinced that this practice would continue. But I am pleased to say that the recipient is sitting amongst us and it is an honour, and a great personal pleasure, to present an award which, to my knowledge, has never before been given to a churchmouse.'

Ole stepped down from the rostrum and undid the red satin bow as Spike got slowly to his feet and moved forward as the eulogy continued.

'With sponsorship from the Leonardo da Vinci Parachute Company I hereby present you with the deeds of Membership, the initials of which can be used after your name and, in addition, you are entitled to wear this hat of honour on all official occasions.'

Ole handed over the deeds and placed the hat, a three-cornered sky blue job with a white fur trim, on Spike's head. His hand was then warmly shaken and he returned, limping slightly and leaning heavily on a stick, to his seat as the gathering enthusiastically clapped his progress.

He had just sat down when he noticed Cheribina smiling at him.

He smiled back.

Angelica heard her sister sniggering and poked her in the ribs.

'What's so funny?' she asked.

'The initials of the Brotherhood make up Brother Spikusbum.'

That set them both off and the disruption that followed caused Ole to postpone his speech regarding Angelica's miraculous recovery until the evening. He quickly thanked all concerned and added that, judging from the applause, the service had certainly been a great success.

Spike managed to avoid being carried shoulder high from the Chantry when he remembered something St Paul said in one of his *Letters to the Corinthians*.

'If the masses want to carry you off, then make sure you know where they're taking you'

He wanted to invite Johanne to the party and found him about to disappear out of the vent and away. The fliegarmaus promised to look in for a noggin, as long as the weather remained fine, but he wouldn't be staying too late as his eyes were still sore and he needed his sleep.

Angelica, herself resplendent in a blue wimple, loved the hat and remembered a story about a handsome PrinceMouse and a glass slipper. She added that Spike looked just like the prince and, if he ever revoked his vows and asked for her hand, then could he please wear that hat.

It was meant as a joke but her sister, plus a few ladymice friends who happened to be within earshot, all awaited his reply with bated breath. Spike's mouth opened and shut several times as a saying, ascribed to the Father of Sir Thomas More, came vividly to mind;

'Marriage is like dipping your hand into a bucket containing twenty snakes and an eel, it's a twenty to one chance that you'll get a snake.'

Ole rescued him from the ear shattering silence to sign some papers and then he scuttled, like a CriminalMouse, back to the safety of his cell. The hat caught a peg on entering and then, kicking off his sandals, he jumped onto the bunk to stretch his arms and think about his new award.

Brother Spikus B.U.M. SpikusBum. Spikesbum!

And he sat bolt upright as he realised what the two ladymice were giggling about!

Ole was locking up the office for the day when Spike arrived, out of breath, to explain the problem but Ole assured him that the committee had already shortened the designated initials and enquired if this abbreviation, *Brother Spikus U.M.,* would be acceptable.

If so could he please carry on home so he could have something to eat and take a nap before the evening activities began!

Spike apologized before agreeing and then, watching the old mouse slowly walk away, decided that Brother Yoric would have a hard act to follow.

Narrator's Note

There were four footnotes in the final part of the journal which were of interest

The first one was that the Fliegermausmedic advised Johanne to wear dark glasses for his ongoing eye problem and this turned into a fashion trend amongst the younger set adding Gothicism to their already Gothic appearance. He had agreed to 'lose' the flying suit on his flight equipment returns to Fliegermaus Command in Transylvania so it was repaired and polished ready for display, together with the parachute and the crosstree, in the Exouris section of the Close Museum.

The second was that Matilda, also earmarked for display, led to a heated discussion between Gerard and Victor on whose name should appear on the 'Built By' plaque. G came before V so, according to one mouse, the plaque should read 'Built by Gerard Du and Victor'.

The majority however felt that it should read the other way around and Victor, who owned the plans after all, even went so far as suggesting that the French mouse's name be left off altogether seeing that he was only a 'bleedin frog'.

'We wouldn't have this problem if I'd left this old fart to spacewalk,' Gerard replied angrily, and added that he would have been the first to hammer the stake through Victor's heart at East Harnham Crossroads.

Victor retaliated by calling him a 'Nihilistical Scumbag'.

Gerard stormed off to look up the meaning in his English/French Dictionary of 'Nasty Things said to French Mice over the Years'.

Unfortunately the page was missing and then, on asking MacDowell and Reggie what it meant, received the collective reply that he was one.

The plaque finally read 'Built by two good mice'.

The third one was that the musical ensemble had developed into quite a polished quintet and received an invitation to play at the annual tea dance of the Salisbury Mousewomen's Embroidery Guild. One could only imagine the stir that Johanne, in full violinatical accord, would create so Ole declined. Margaret's remark that no one took her dancing led to Ole promising that Linemouse Dancing would be on their retirement agenda!

And the final one concerned the 'end of term' party. Everyone seemed to have had a good skin-full of 'Ecclesiastical Punch' with Angelica putting on quite a show with Sean MacNab. Lisa, and then Margaret, commenced a hand standing exhibition which attracted a lot of interest from the males once they had divested themselves of their knickers. Cheribina was holding court, with TC her most attentive consort, discussing the latest trends in Classical Boroque and the cat was feeling extra happy as he'd been assured that his earlier misdemeanour had been erased from the Asbos Diptych.

Ole tried his best to keep the four friends in line, telling stories of alcoholic churchmice he had known, but when Reggie told him he was wasting his time he joined them mainly to avoid confronting Margaret about her wayward and disgraceful behaviour.

Victor, according to the latest newsflash, was still making his way down from the steeple and expected to arrive at midday by which time everyone would have packed up and gone home. It was a well-known fact that he took ages to get ready!

Johanne arrived somewhat later, landing a little way away and walking the rest, and was accompanied by his FliegerFrauMaus. This surprised everyone as he'd never mentioned a partner but everyone made Gladys, who spoke Englishspeake fluently having spent some time in Torquay as an Au Pair to the Devon branch of the Munster Family, very welcome.

Angelica and Lisa were most impressed with her dress and shoes.

And finally Salisbury Cathedral itself forming a backdrop to yet another generation of characters and standing at peace with the world.

Clive Russell, F.Sc.
Barford St Martin
8th August 2000

Narrator's End Notes

That just about wraps up the narration of the first journal. It was finished on the 8th of the 8th of the year 0 and I've spent all this time editing it into some sort of form suitable for human scrutiny that has certainly speeded up an ageing process so obvious in the graying of hair and the dimming of eye. It's been hard graft but this is one of the few tasks I've actually finished, and which entitles me to have the letters, *'half-hearted'*, erased from my memorial.

There are two more journals, plus his sketchbook, sitting on the shelf awaiting my attention. I've started the next one but do I have the *wherewithal* to tackle the third?

Somehow I think not.

A leaflet ended up on my doormat last week and it was from an undertaking firm offering pre-paid funeral plans.

Plan 'A' covered the basic cost and a plain, but adequate, box.

Plan 'B', in addition to that above, included a *'Necrophilia Skip'*.

This unusual addition to the norm is explained as follows;

The Doctor is called, the required forms are signed, and he leaves. Next comes the Undertaker who collects, and departs, with the newly departed. The skip then arrives and is placed with due dignity, by a team of moonlighting fireman suitably rigged out in dark suits and top hats, adjacent to the back door.

The soiled sheets and underwear, together with treasured family mementos lovingly accumulated by the oldies over the years and which usually end up at the tip anyway, are placed in the skip and collected within 12 hours by the same m/f (or the blue watch).

This plan eases a heavy burden from the shoulders of their grieving children, Chloe and Honeysuckle, who have taken the minimal time off from their high-powered positions in America to fly in for the funeral. They can then rummage through the remaining pickings, in a peaceful and uncluttered atmosphere, to select their desires before the stretch limo arrives to take them to the airport, later that same day, and return them whence they came.

I do hope this will not be the fate of these journals.

Clive Russell, F.Sc.
Barford St Martin
31st January 2002

The final revelations

This Rev Aaron Buzacott Jnr gave a brief outline of the deceased's life and mentioned that the loss of the limb was a casualty of one of the earlier European wars. He went on to say that it had been quickly pickled in brine and was believed to be still in the crypt of the parish church at the owner's birthplace of Upton in Norfolk.

A sketch of the coracle showed that it folded up into a leather suitcase and I then realised that this type of boat only needed one arm to propel it!

The rest of the letter was religious and at the bottom of the last page was the logo of CA Williams and the fact that he was a signatory under the American Guano Act of 1856.

I have narrated the first journal and I'm halfway through the second one but I haven't come across anything further on William Stickman. However I did meet an ancient Royal Marine cornet player (retired) who, when he joined the service as a lad many years ago, remembered hearing about a secret section within the Marines. After some debacle during the Russia-Japanese War of 1905, the section was disbanded and all details erased from Naval Records.

Evidently the section was on loan to the Russian Fleet at the time, in return for favours done or expected no doubt, and it consisted of combatants who had lost an arm in battle but were still assessed as good fighting men. It was known as the 'One Armed Raiding Party' (OARPs), and comprised of six men with good right arms, and six with good left arms, going into battle in close formation, empty shoulder to empty shoulder, swinging cutlasses with their good arms like whirling dervishes. They proved to be a formidable foe, winning many battle honours along the way, and some marines were so desperate to join this elite band of men that they even went so far as to disable an arm on purpose.

This practice was frowned upon by the Naval Authorities who found that, on the eve of an important battle, they had twice as many lefts as rights. A third of the unit therefore had to sit out on the reserve benches desperately hoping that the next casualty would be a lefter.

The particular skirmish that led to the unit being disbanded happened in Port Arthur when the Japanese Guerrillas, cunning devils that they were, mounted a frontal attack in arrowhead formation that penetrated the lightly protected armless centre. The bugler immediately sounded 'Reverse Close Order Formation' which turned the lefters towards the rear, the righters swung towards the front so, when someone shouted 'Charge', the unit went round in a circle and sustained many casualties amongst themselves.

It was a sad day for England when the bodies, piled high on the Pinnace Boats flying their Jacks at half mast, were returned to the British Fleet completely stripped of their dignity, and anything of value on their persons, by the accompanying Russian Sailors.

One final story that may interest you and then I'll finish

Rev John Williams, that stalwart of the London Missionary Society, set off from Tahiti in 1818 for the Hervey Islands but was blown off course and commenced operations in Raiatea in the Society Islands. He ended up in a cannibals cooking pot in Vanuatu and, even as his lightly spiced and medium rare left thigh was being enjoyed by a family named Oijiah, he summoned his faith and strength to call out.

The family nodded their heads, as they assumed he was asking how they were enjoying him, when in fact he was preaching; 'Forgive them Lord for they know not what they do!'

Their collective nodding heads could possibly have gone a certain way in pacifying him as he died, peacefully enough considering the circumstances, just as they started on the right thigh.

R.I.P.

Definitely the final note

I was cogitating one day in the Close when a baglady approached and sat beside me. We got talking and she told me that her great grandfather had renovated William Russell's House in Queen's Street. From somewhere within her person a roll of old canvas appeared and she offered it to me for a pound.

Wanted for Questioning

Brother Spikus

The Renegade Chapter ChurchMouse to assist The Ecclesiastical Authorities with their enquiries about the unlawful springing of an Itinerant YiddisherMouse held in Lawful Custody at the Salisbury Cathedral Lock-Up.

This drawing was wrapped inside and I took it to 'the man who knows all'. Evidently the house once belonged to Thomas Harding, a Clerk of Works at the Cathedral who, in 1470, gave the house to the Clergy. In the 1520s the house gave shelter to 'Seven Poore Artists' while in the 1530s St Osmond's Tomb, plus masses of books and artfacts, were destroyed.

Maybe the vandals missed the house and this drawing somehow survived!

I subsequently felt encouraged to narrate the next journal which opens with a 'Good Samaritan' deed by Spike whilst he was out jogging. This simple act was the first link in a chain of events that initially called into question his faith, then rapidly deteriorates to a point where he heads the 'Most Wanted' lists throughout Wessex and continues corkscrewing rapidly downwards when he's exiled from his adopted country to embark on a pilgrimage towards Santiago del Compestella.

His travelling companion is Elias, a fellow ecclesiasticalite with a serious addidiction in the eyes of Yiddisher Law, and who should really be heading towards Jerusalem in the opposite direction on his quest to 'find oneself'.

They land at St Malo, detour off to Burgos in an effort to address Elias' problem with the help of a cousin, the mysterious Uncle Shmiel who resides in the area, before continuing along 'The Way' on a journey that's not uneventful.

I will do my best to finish the narration, and get into print, *Opening Gambit 2* before the Good Lord calls me!

Appendices

Gerard Du, on his return to Chartres after his Sabbatical in 1529, first noticed the Unhappiest Angel slumped forelornly on her plinth during one of his early morning stroll&nosearounds. She had lost an arm and a wing during the Ecclesiastical Skirmishes of earlier years and spares were difficult to come by even if one could afford them. Gerald then made a point to stop by most mornings, when he was in residence and it wasn't raining, to recount his Salisbury Adventures to a captive audience of one. She initially straightened up, and then cracked a grin that soon developed into her famous smile and this, so I believe, is still in place to this very day.